HATE: A ROMANCE

by the same author

The Image

HATE: A ROMANCE

Tristan Garcia

Translated from the French
by Marion Duvert and Lorin Stein

faber and faber

Originally published in France in 2008
by Éditions Gallimard as *La Meilleure Part des hommes*
First published in the US in 2010
by Faber and Faber, Inc.
First published in the UK in 2011
by Faber and Faber Ltd
Bloomsbury House
74–77 Great Russell Street
London WC1B 3DA

Printed in England by CPI Mackays, Chatham

A CIP record for this book
is available from the British Library

ISBN 978–0–571–25183–4

2 4 6 8 10 9 7 5 3 1

To my four parents, whom I love equally

To Agnès

The characters in this novel have never existed other than in the pages of this book.

If, however, the reader feels that in certain ways they resemble real persons whom he or she knows, or knows of, that is simply because other persons or characters would behave no differently under similar conditions.

THE FOUR
OF US

1

WILLIE

William Miller, in the photos he showed me, looks like a subdued little kid, well-behaved and dull.

He was born in Amiens, in 1970, where he always told me he spent a childhood that seemed happy at the time and terribly sad in retrospect. He had an open face and thick eyebrows. He was a slow student—to put it bluntly, he was no genius—and the one time I heard him describe a memory of first grade, it was of always having to pee and being made fun of. He was a bed wetter. Otherwise there was nothing especially martyrlike about him.

His father, an Ashkenazi Jew, was in the garment business. He opened a shop in Amiens near the *mairie* which failed, so he went to work as a salesman in a department store selling linens.

His mother was a housewife.

William had two brothers, I never knew their names. He was the youngest. He was still little when he started wearing glasses. His parents got divorced when he was ten. William stayed with his mother in their house near Étouvie. His father moved into an apartment. William didn't see him after that, or not much of him anyway. They weren't close. His father, when he had to take him for the weekend, used to leave him with his aunt, in Compiègne, where William liked to pretend he was a king or a knight in the ruins of the castle, sticking close to the parking lot.

One day we were talking about it, in a leather banquette near the bar. He was winding his big silver watch, fiddling with his wig, he was laughing, and I remember him saying, "At the time I thought it was normal, I didn't feel good or bad, if you see what I mean. Now that I've been around a little, I realize it was wretched."

He was smiling. His brothers were tall—the older one, I think, works for the city, the second one had run away, he ended up in reform school, then the army. From the age of eight or nine, all through William's adolescence, he basically had no communication with them, except when one of them asked what was in the fridge. He got fat.

"Looking back, you realize how many silences there were in a house like that, where the love had just broken in two, you know. Like a string . . ."

He played tennis. It was his father who signed him up to play sports. He didn't like his body, he'd have rather they left him alone. He wasn't much good, and he spent hours at a time in the toilet. As the years went by he started to have a few friends, all girls. He made friends with some boys, it's true, in grade school, he said, but never anything deep. There was this one boy, Guillaume, who he practiced tennis with on Sundays, but then Guillaume moved east for vocational school. He had red hair, he never talked, he had no sense of balance on a bike. There'd been a couple of birthday parties, at his house. That was pretty much it.

He was crazy about *Star Wars*, it became a real obsession. He was always dreaming about Chewbacca and the Ewoks and their planet, and the Empire, and the *Millennium Falcon* and bipods, the AT-STs at the base on Hoth. He told me once, when the prequels finally came out twenty years later, "That was my way of being a boy."

Whenever the doorbell rang, his mother would call out, "Don't open it, you don't know who it is." Maybe this was because of the scandal that erupted, before the divorce, when his father's mistress burst into their house in a rage, her red hair wild.

William often got phone calls from girls, he always loved to act as a confidant—so he said. But if you ask me, I never saw him really *listen* to anyone: he was always the one who talked. His friends just tried to keep up.

In *lycée* he kept to himself, and he got mediocre grades. You could see the red pen on his compositions ("messy") and his report cards ("fair"). They put him in the economics and social sciences track, and the next thing he knew he'd got his *bac* without even having asked for it. He had longish hair back then—not like anyone's in particular, it wasn't as if he had some idol who wore it that way. At least, I doubt it. He just didn't go to the barber. And he wore button-downs. He had that cupid's bow which everyone would fall in love with, later on, and which back then was covered with peach fuzz. To be blunt, it wasn't a very good look—even clean, somehow it looked grubby. He listened to classical music compilations and French variety songs. He started to read poetry because of a teacher; then he discovered rock, but never really explored it. He liked dance music, but not dancing. If you asked about those years, he wouldn't try to explain, just shrug. "What did I *like*? . . ." I don't think he knew where he belonged.

He didn't start hating his father all at once. It happened in stages. He learned to express himself by running his father down, little by little at first, to other people, to strangers he met. He took a little room in student housing. He enrolled in a program studying sales.

At first he fit in, more or less. He was a little too shy, but he knew enough to smile if you tapped him on the shoulder. He was a bad talker—but in a nice way. An interesting way. He had big, hairy hands, which he was embarrassed about. He felt uncomfortable wearing a tie, and yet sometimes he could be sharp, he was lively, and he could clean up nicely when he had to.

"You're like a butterfly coming out of its cocoon, William. Soon you'll spread your wings." That's what his boss told him during his first internship. Will's admiration for this guy was boundless: he was a bon vivant, a dynamic personality, someone who'd mastered life. When he snapped his fingers it had the force of truth.

Will never understood what happened, though he worried and worried about it. Something occurred between them, something scandalous and wrong, even if no one ever knew. So William left Amiens, he was barely nineteen, in 1989, the year the Berlin Wall came down—but as he liked to say, what side did it fall on?

"What did the Wall come down to? Really, I'm asking."

He stumbled off to Paris, Gare du Nord—no job, no nothing. Less than nothing.

He met Doum a year and a half later, in June.

2
DOUMÉ

Dominique Rossi had always looked handsome in a mature way, responsible and lightly chiseled by time. The trouble was, when he was twenty it didn't suit him. He had to wait to look his age.

The village he came from lies just next to Calenzana, in Corsica, a few kilometers from L'Île-Rousse and Calvi. His father was a doctor, the big doctor in town. He had five older brothers, no sisters. He was the baby.

His mother? Italian. That's where he got his long black eyelashes, and the rest of it. A person could have done worse.

He grew up in a big house at the foot of the mountains. Winters they went skiing in the Alps, summers they spent in Sicily then Tunisia, where they owned beautiful second, third, etc., houses.

The ties between his father, Pascal, and the separatists were never entirely clear. He was an intellectual of sorts and in later years he often, you might say, shepherded the young men who started to organize in the early seventies. He owned a vast library, and in his own way exposed the young Bastiais to the idea that Corsica had always been, historically, under foreign domination. Except when Paoli, that slick . . . well, but that was another story and it ended with the French. Pascal Rossi was never partisan in anything. No, he was a dilettante, a blowhard with a great thick beard, who smoked his pipe and reflected on events. He spoke

Corsican because he taught himself out of a book. He wanted to be able to talk with the old people. He encouraged the younger generation to reconnect with their language, he showed them all the ways the mainland exploited the island, more and more, without bringing them infrastructure or jobs. Unemployment was already on the rise.

Dominique remembered them sitting there in the upstairs room with the wood paneling: Alain, François, Jean-Claude, and the other Alain. His father never said their last names. He'd say, "Read the papers, you know who they are." They were a few years older. Dominique would sit in the corner, he wasn't allowed to drink with them. Wrapped up in her shawl, his mother kept an eye on him—when it came to things like that, she was as strict as his father was relaxed.

Then came Aléria, the underground resistance, and the founding of the FLNC. They say it was his father who opened the door to Jean-Claude, not long afterward, the night of the shoot-out. He certainly didn't approve of the underground tactics, of armed resistance. He never had. Jean-Claude was one of the fugitives on the wanted poster. That famous poster. When the original Bastiais started fighting among themselves, he'd shot the other Alain on his motorbike, who'd lately gotten into bed with the Communists, over some imbroglio having to do with the purge of Orsini. And for Pascal Rossi, the second Alain had been like a son, a sixth son.

"He was like something out of the Bible," Dominique would sigh.

I never could follow the ins and outs of these stories.

Pascal Rossi had opened the door of his barn, where he'd gone to do the chores. Here was Jean-Claude, who had just murdered Alain, on the lam. He'd turned up here by chance looking for help, having crossed the *maquis*. He had no idea he was on the property of Pascal Rossi, Alain's "father," his protector. Jean-Claude stood there petrified. If it had been anyone else . . .

Pascal Rossi let him in and tended to his wounds. He was per-fectly plain: "You were wrong to kill Alain. I ought to turn you in, but I'll give you till tomorrow at noon before I call the cops. Hear me? You can sleep and have something to eat. Tomorrow, though, if I have to help them hunt you down myself, I'll do it. And you know it."

"My father had known him since he was little, is the thing . . ."

Jean-Claude was killed a month later. They say Pascal wasn't far away when it happened.

Doumé pursed his lips: "That's how it is with this 'Corsican hospitality,' you know. I never had time for it, all those males playing at manly honor, everyone hugging and kissing, all this business about respect, then they turn around and kill you and it's all part of the Code. The fucking Code. Compared to that, communism is feminine. It's more theoretical, more sensitive."

At seventeen he left for the mainland, for Nice, where he at-tended *lycée* and prepared for the École Normale. None of the universities was ever controlled by the separatists, especially not Corte. In the seventies all the militants went to study in Nice. Doum couldn't stand them. They were always talking to him about his father, and his father was always talking to him about them.

Dominique worked alone. He worked hard, he worked con-scientiously, and during those years he moved closer and closer to the leftists. That way he wouldn't have to betray the young militants around him, but wouldn't have to switch off his brain and join them, either.

He was suffocating.

"Nice was just more of the island. Beautiful, sure, but I didn't get anything out of it. Except maybe Place Masséna."

When he got in to one of the *grandes écoles*, he went up to Paris. Paris was another story. He'd smile just thinking about it. "So I had a square Corsican face, and bad skin, but it wasn't all that bad. And, well, I'd already gone out with a couple of girls."

"My first time was in Paris, in the suburbs, the place belonged to the girl's father. We did it next to the china, on a folding cot, practically underneath the sideboard. Christ, what a memory."

He shrugged. "I don't remember much about it, actually. I do remember washing the dishes afterward. Putting away the silver. Housekeeping, coupledom, you know how it is. A trap—I could see it even then."

I nodded.

"I pretty much dropped out when I became an activist. But I'd already learned a thing or two. I'd mastered rhetoric as a threat. I knew how to use theory as blackmail. I held on to that and it came in handy. It was an asset. Back then, you might say, I used my skills for the class struggle, all the stuff I'd learned in my father's upstairs sitting room, the room with the paneling. My God, just imagine. The Party. Or as we liked to call it, the Organization. For two, three years of my life it meant everything to me. Then I was done. Were we believers? Sure, we believed. But afterward, you know, in the eighties, with Stand and the rest of it, there was no question of belief. No, that's what we really *were*, we were defending what we were. All we wanted was to exist. That's a big difference, compared to the Organization, where we were fighting for ideas. We believed in those ideas, absolutely. But an idea's just an idea, you see what I'm saying—we weren't fighting for our bodies.

"In terms of ideology, our leader was a guy named Elias. After Overnay, I mean after he got killed, we spent a long time debating whether to take up arms—as if the whole thing wasn't already over and done with. Elias was pro-violence. Daniel, who handled politics and concrete action—insofar as anything was concrete back in those days, when all anybody ever talked about was 'praxis' and no one ever actually *did* anything remotely practical—at any rate, Daniel was against it. He dissolved the Party, he started another one, which turned into a club, or really more like a kind of nonprofit, two years later. It was more what I guess you'd call traditional. The swing voters backed the Socialists before the victory of '81.

"I voted for Mitterrand myself.

"Three years later Elias, keeper of the flame of liberation, tactician of hand-to-hand combat, grand strategist of the avant-garde convergence—this guy who said we should all spend a lot of time thinking about why the nonthinkers (that is, the workers) were always in the right, who said we ought to be educating them so they could show us the way forward, which supposedly was all part of the dialectic, but mostly just meant getting our asses kicked outside some factory gate, this guy Elias . . . but how can I describe him? He was the kind of guy who'd quote Marx at you whenever you tried to talk, who'd quote Lenin when you quoted Marx, Liebknecht when you quoted Lenin, Pannekoek when you quoted Liebknecht, Mandel when you quoted Pannekoek, and Mao when you ended up quoting Mandel—and when you quoted Mao, he gave you some worker from Billancourt . . . and if you were a worker from Billancourt, he shut you up with Lenin. You get the picture.

"So anyway, I lived in terror of the guy. I felt almost guilty around him, this man who stood for the proletariat, the downtrodden, and the antifascist movement all in his own person, which at the same time was ironic, since he was the son of a big industrialist, a specialist in African timber . . . In any case, two years later he got religion, of all things . . ."

Doumé laughed. "Though I suppose he had religion all along.

"Unless you count a couple of 'interventions,' the Party never did a damn thing in Paris. Three years of doing nothing. There was nothing for me to learn, though it helped me for what came later. It helped me for life.

"When the Party fell apart, a couple of flakes, people none of us really knew, took off for the southwest and continued the

resistance by kidnapping the head of some chamber of com-
merce, this big fat guy from Gers who had no idea what was going on, and then afterward, to liberate some funds—they were
completely broke—they knocked over a Crédit Agricole in Pau,
and they killed a cop without even meaning to. They spent a
year and a half going from barn to barn in the Hautes-Pyrénées
before they got caught in their hideout. In the end it was a couple of day-trippers who turned them in. They're still doing time.
He has cancer, she's basically lost her mind.

"Elias became Orthodox. He started writing commentaries
on the Torah. Daniel made a deal with the Socialists, he lobbied
the Party to support Mitterrand, and they got three posts in the
head office. He ended up as secretary of tourism and land man-
agement, then Fabius came along and they resigned. And came
back later on.

"And me, well, I was in New York . . . And that's how it ended,
the Organization, the Party, the left—well, in any case the left as
we knew it—and all that kind of thing. Though in reality it had
all been over for years, long before we came around. Oh yeah,
and Leibo, Leibo went off to write his books, and then he ended
up—well, but I don't need to tell you about Leibo.

"Someone's always passing around some petition for the ones
who are still in prison. A petition to set them free, hell, what is
it, a quarter century later. The poor fuckups.

"I sign, naturally. Leibo, too, sometimes I see his name. I mean,
what else are you going to do?

"But by then I was long gone. I'd met the photographer, you
know. We took off for New York—and I mean this was back
when New York was still New York. That was an eye-opener, let
me tell you.

"It blew my fucking mind."

3

LEIBO

Jean-Michel Leibowitz, I believe, would have liked to be remembered as a philosopher but have lived a life of power and action. He chose a middle road, and so was always profoundly unhappy. I think he read Tintin, I think he loved reading Tintin, he might have grown up to be a journalist. And then, later on, he began to look down on comic books . . . Even so, he wrote for the papers, a lot. When he was fourteen he read Stendhal for the love stories, Mathilde de la Mole and the rest of it. He was an idealist.

He was Jewish, and his father always told him, "Son, you have a French first name. That means you're French." The word *Jew* was never spoken. Not until years later, and hardly even then.

When he read Spinoza, Jean-Michel naturally understood none of it. That's to be expected. But he understood that it was something beyond him, and that it was something he would attain. Philosophy—the dream of a lifetime. That's the kind of kid he was.

A good student. A very, very good student.

They lived in Aubervilliers, him, his father, and his mother. His parents had been Gaullists, then they supported Mitterrand. His father left early in the morning for work. Sometimes he worked nights. He didn't drink, he didn't belong to the union, he cursed his fellow workmen who showed up drunk, he wore a suit and never put on his blue smock until he got to the plant.

His mother would clear the dishes off the oilcloth. Jean-Michel would drink hot chocolate. His mother didn't talk much, so he read.

His father would come home, he'd hang up his coat in the front hall, he'd tousle Jean-Michel's hair. "My son the book-worm . . ."

Jean-Michel spent a lot of time in the local library, and he played soccer and rode a bike. He liked Malraux.

He once mentioned that the first time he jacked off was to *Madame Bovary*.

Judging from the pictures I've seen, he kept his hair short, but it was kinky and wouldn't stay combed. He used to talk a lot about his parents, very little about his childhood.

Jean-Michel left home to do his preparatory studies. He worked hard, he worked a lot, he worked all night. He drank, he wore a trench coat.

"Men have no secrets. You'd think they would, but in the end a life hides nothing. At the end of the day, we see it all and we're disappointed. The problem is how to make ourselves believe that some mystery remains" (quoted from *Fragments of an Unfinished Work: Portraits from Memory*). If you know Jean-Michel the way I do, his life story is all of a piece. All you can do is nod in agreement: It's all so *him*.

At any rate, Jean-Michel Leibowitz did his *khâgne* at Henri IV, which he attended on scholarship. There he met all his future friends, his future supporters, his publisher, and even his enemies; he was, I believe, brilliant.

He loved adventurers. At some point he'd given up playing soccer. According to his first girlfriend he looked a little like the striker Dominique Rocheteau, the "Green Angel" of Saint-Étienne. He hit the books.

"I've lived a frustrated life; if I'd become what I wanted to be as a child, I would be one of the men I hate today, and who hate me, but who nevertheless filled the dreams of my childhood." So he writes in his inimitable style, a style not unlike his hair, in *The Fate of a Generation*. You see, that pretty much says it all.

In point of fact, he played at being an adventurer himself, in his own small way. He became a leftist. And did nothing. As a student at the École Normale Supérieure of the late seventies, he took his place in the tail of the comet that was the Maoist movement. He didn't smoke, but he did wear his hair long, and by then Sartre was already over and done with and had faded from the scene. Elias was in charge of the Fifth Arrondissement cell of the UPCIF—don't ask me what it stands for. Althusser's influence was on the wane, he just kept shuffling the same old mimeographs on the Communist Party, and besides he had his domestic troubles, as we know. *Libération* was in its heyday, with Serge July and the rest of the original staff, before they all quit. Leibowitz was close to Elias, though he didn't go in for the religion thing. He participated, a little, in meetings, manifestos, and sit-ins. You might say he made connections. Twenty-five years later he hangs around with the same people—just in a different setting.

Leibowitz met Doumé, I mean Dominique, who was always hanging around the École Normale, and they also knew each other through the Organization.

"I was a leftist back then, like everyone else." Note the past tense.

He went off to teach in the States, originally as a graduate student. When he came back he was still a man of the left, but he'd stopped being a leftist. He'd done a lot of reading, he'd seen things, he'd gotten to know the Jewish left of New York, he now understood that communism couldn't make room for certain realities, certain things that transcended society—religions, nations, communities . . . That was how he put it.

Also, he'd met Sara. They got married in 1980.

The first time he went on TV, in the late seventies, because neither Deleuze, nor Lévi-Strauss, nor Vidal-Naquet, the men of the hour, wanted to do it, he appeared on a "literary" program— meaning the set involved bookshelves—to talk about Solzhenitsyn and totalitarianism. He was a philosopher. He never finished his dissertation. He went straight into teaching and writing.

At the time he'd written this little book, *The Hydra of Power*, taking the Eastern Bloc dissidents to task. It wasn't enough to fight the hard power inherent in so-called Communist societies, which in fact represented nothing more than totalitarian capitalism; one had to denounce the soft power in so-called liberal societies as well. This was an insidious power that surrounded us on a daily basis, an individualized power that, above and beyond any traditional, familial, economic, or social structures, incorporated itself in us, which is to say literally integrated itself into our bodies, personalized itself as a fetish object through advertising, ideology, and the productions of high culture, thus what one had to fight against was the cultural power of the institutionalized class system . . . blah blah blah, all the mandatory words. The pamphlet never went into a second printing. It wasn't brainless, it was the times he lived in.

It's history now.

I remember him turning around the night I asked him about the book. I was trying to understand. He cleared his throat, he frowned, he pushed his glasses back on his nose. He had a way of making you feel guilty when he was in the wrong, and was always happy to try his luck from a false position.

"I was right—or rather, I was wrong in the right way.

"I always chose the opposing side, in everything. In soccer, when I took a penalty kick, I'd think the goalie was going to dive left, so I'd better shoot to the right. But then I'd think the goalie would end up thinking that I was thinking of shooting to the right, and so I'd better shoot left. But if he thought I was going to shoot to the other side, then I'd have to shoot to the other side of the other side, precisely where he was expecting me to shoot. I'd shoot to the right—but it had all that thinking be-hind it, you see what I mean?"

"And he caught it?"

"Who?"

"What do you mean, who? The goalie."

"Oh, I don't remember."

"Ah."

"The point, Liz, is that I was always aiming the other way, always fighting the current. You have to fight the current, you know, of the times you live in."

In other words, he was an intellectual.

That was him all over: Jean-Michel Leibowitz, Leibo. The Leib.

4

ME

As for me? My name is Elizabeth Levallois. I'm Willie's friend, Doumé's colleague, Leibo's lover.

I'm thirty-three, a journalist. My face is long and, I think, rather pretty. I believe in pills. I know how to dress, but I have a mind of my own. I suppose you could say I'm a bitch. Furthermore, I suppose 90 percent of the population, if they met me, would roll their eyes and say, "One of *those*." Fair enough. I'm the kind of person one comes across in Paris. I have a nice apartment. I'm not rich, but definitely not poor, and I'm left-wing because I still cling to too many illusions to be a cynic. I am what you might call well-bred. I've never been married. My jackets fit, I choose nice things, I know how to make myself agreeable. I have some education. My father is in publishing, my mother— well, Maman's a free spirit, a hippie of sorts. She had a singing career, for a while. She left. I got a stepmother in her place. Whatever. I was always in awe of my father. To my detriment, clearly. He was a connoisseur, an actor, the sort of person who knows everyone, who can be anything. I have had trouble with love. There've been older men, professors, a politician (short), a boss (medium-sized), and Leibo. I am awfully fond of Leibo. We've had ten years of adultery, of rendezvous, of getaways. What else should you know? I always thought it would be nice to be a redhead. (My hair is brown.) I wear two rings, I can talk on my feet, I can drink.

I attended Sciences-Po, as we people generally do. I attended a Parisian *lycée*. My first love played guitar in a band, hardly a good sign. This was, after all, the mid-eighties. Last I heard, he'd become a junkie. I was more careful. I'll still smoke a joint now and then, but that's about it. I've maintained a few punk-chic connections, if you know what I mean, for the parties. Then came the professor of French. The nights out with girlfriends, wild nights, the net that spins itself around you without your ever noticing the threads, until one day you reach saturation: there's no one left to meet, not really. There's a threshold and you've crossed it.

At Sciences-Po, yes, he was brilliant. Jean-Michel Leibowitz, the Leib. Though, in hindsight, I don't think he was much of a thinker. He was a product of his times—and who isn't, you say. He'd say the same. A clever, unhappy man. I seem to have a weakness for the forty-something routine: I'm wretched, I've been wounded by life, and so on. Midlife crisis as come-on. Perhaps it's some sort of maternal instinct. So we played cat and mouse for five, six, seven years, each convinced that we'd found the love of our lives. He was my mentor. Then we slept together, and that was that.

I went to work for *Libé*. I covered "culture," that is, everything and nothing. I had my little supplement. I went out, I kept up with the scene. Television was my first beat. It's how everyone starts out. I'd go hear shows, indie rock shows, to compensate for the shit I watched on TV. I did trend pieces, I wrote up the latest thing. It leaves a funny taste in your mouth. You smell death in the life all around you, and all the while you keep waiting for something new. I did "fashion," too, naturally, and "books" every now and then. If we were sitting across a dinner table and you asked me, I could tell you what people were talking about; I couldn't tell you much else, but I knew what was *current*.

All of which Leibo loathed. He was always going on about the *un*fashionable, the "nonmodern," the old days. Our arguments now strike me as terribly simple. Too simple. He's shorter than I am. When we were in bed, the sheet didn't cover my breasts. He taught me well, in class, about memory, the old days, the Other, silence, and history—I retained it. Come to think of it, I stand for the exact opposite: each new fad supplanting the last. When it was his turn and Leibo came back into style, he liked to say, I'd have no choice but to embrace his views—it's all I was pro-grammed to do. It used to turn him on, lecturing me and crying in my arms.

The eternal question was whether I'd have a kid. Fashion comes and goes. It was like flipping a coin: I'll have one, I won't have one. Leibo has three children of his own.

I have green eyes. They're beautiful, I'm told. It's not as if Leibo was all I had. From time to time I slept with other men. But I am, all things considered, a faithful person.

I met Willie at a B-list party. He'd dashed off a piece for my little magazine, which covered the arts, music, and new media. I slept with him—literally, in the same bed, nothing else of course. That was never his thing. I was his confidante—this, too, in the literal sense, entailing nights of despair, two a.m. phone calls, talking him down off the ledge, mopping up the blood, washing him, feeding him like a baby until he disappeared for three weeks. Three weeks when, you see, he was *happy*.

As it happens, I was the one who introduced Doum to Willie. By then I was working with Doum. We'd cowrite the last-minute fillers, the *coups d'humeur*. We shared an office. He was a fixture at the paper. He brought me on. He was my godfather.

Doum's tough, and he enjoys a fight. There were maybe a dozen times when we really had it out. Then he'd come in, with-out a word, and there'd be a package on my desk, earrings. That meant it was over, he'd made up with me. Doum always loved me in earrings. "Liz," he liked to say, "it's a sex thing."

I'd watch TV at home for work. I didn't have much time

alone. My days were hectic. I had to juggle the times when Leibo was free to see me, the job, nights, going out, Sundays, meals, articles. Vacations.

I always draw two lines on my eyelids. That's my good-luck charm. I read too much. I don't have a favorite book; that's for people who don't do it for a living. Soon I'll be forty, it happens to everyone. I have my own reputation for toughness. Now and then I forgive. I have noticed that, when people have something against you, they can be wonderfully blind to your troubles, to the possibility that you may sometimes have problems of your own.

I have a nose for things.

Also: high cheekbones, difficult wiry hair, legs a tiny bit soft in the calves. I work out. I diet, sort of. What will become of me? In this world some people are distinct individuals while others are no more than paths of transmission. At my age, the signs are unmistakable: I belong in category two. I have my work cut out for me.

I really loved Willie. He was category one. It's time he had his due, for better or worse. I've been quiet long enough. And me? I'll be there for him, one last time.

JOY AND DISEASE

5

The eighties were a cultural and intellectual wasteland except when it came to TV, free-market economics, and Western homosexuality. Dominique Rossi was not the least bit interested in free-market economics. TV was something he'd watch later on.

What he missed most was their joie de vivre. He was always saying that. Whether gay liberation marked an unprecedented turn in human evolution or whether it was part of some kind of historical cycle, I have no idea.

"It wasn't much like ancient Greece," Doumé would joke, sipping his bourbon, "and it had nothing at all to do with Oscar Wilde."

He was in New York, he was in London, he was in Paris.

"In retrospect, of course, I see that those were the years when cash took on a social democratic value, when the stock market, appearances, surface, cheap crap, bad taste all stuck their tongue out and made a great big face at the planet. An aesthetic based on neon ads and early Atari, desktop publishing and synthesizers. On trash."

Doumé burst out laughing. "For us, it was all the color of love—but I admit that if I'd been straight, it would pretty much have looked like the end of intelligent life and the color of hell.

"But back then I was getting laid, and everyone was dancing. No, it wasn't dumb. Far from it. We'd walk around in broad daylight, we had a blast, we had this sense of belonging. We were a community, but it felt like a universe, not a prison. That changed over time. At the end of the day, you realize it all boils down to the same thing."

Dominique would always look at his pills before he took them. How many times had he found himself back on that crummy old cherry red sofa, cross-legged next to the stereo. He lost himself in thought.

That photographer took him to Le Palace. My God, he'd never felt anything like it. There he was, a bespectacled little student, in his little button-down—even if he was well built, still you always feel like a kid your first time—and he went walking down the hallway, the sound bouncing off the walls, most of all that bass, it got you right in the gut; he felt as if he were making his way between the colonnades and soldiers of some ancestral time, walking toward an arena. It was violent, it hurt, but already he had the pleasure of thinking that maybe it was *about to* feel good, in a second. He ventured out onto the dance floor, the music grabbed you in your stomach, he actually thought he was going to throw up, then he realized it was better to let the music swallow you like a giant heart that was making everybody, all of us, live and vibrate, in unison. He'd forgotten all about Shostakovich, Fauré, bop, and post-punk, everything he knew. This music was alive, it was unbridled, free and constraining at the same time, dressed up and indecent. He learned to dance with his hands in the air then, later, with his pants around his ankles. He learned, as one does, that he was a body. He experimented, on his body. He danced—it wasn't fun at first, because he thought about it, then he forgot and it was good because it wasn't just good anymore, no, it was so much more than good. Nothing else mattered.

And how he used to come!

"Shit, the way we could *come*, back then, I don't think anybody comes that way nowadays."

He laughed softly, he said he sounded like an old fart, an old fart who refused to grow up. You couldn't judge him, he was too self-aware. Except when it came to one thing. Just one.

"What was so joyful about it, it wasn't just the music, the *house nation*, or the disco back before that, or the fucking around. It was everything: the friendship, the philosophy, the clothes, the body hair, the food, the colors. That joie de vivre was everywhere. What made it all the more fun was that it seemed so political. We'd ditched the political parties, Trotsky, the discussions, the 'workers.' It was sexy, you know what I'm saying? You fucked and that was political. You kissed a guy, that was your own October Revolution. It was individual, private—but because we were queer, the private was public. We didn't even need to dick around with demonstrations or sit around discussing union tactics. We screwed, we loved one another, even, and it was more political than any-thing going on in the Assemblée. Sure, it ended up being a kind of free-market economy, with everything privatized, individual-ized. But at the time . . . shit, I sound like a fucking veteran."

He smiled.

He pursed his lips, fiddled with the tape recorder. He was used to it. In the eighties he used to do profiles for the paper. Cul-ture and politics. He covered nightlife and minority causes.

"That word, *minority* . . . That was the good side of democ-racy, wasn't it? The moment where all you had to do was be in a minority and somehow, paradoxically, you were in possession of the truth.

"The photographer dumped me. What did I care? It's not as if we believed in couples back then. It was our sixties, our sexual liberation. Then came Ecstasy . . . We were out of our minds, ab-solutely out of our fucking minds . . . Not that I'd have wanted it to go on that way forever, necessarily.

"I just wouldn't have wanted it to end the way it did. Looking back, that poisons the whole thing, you know?"

Doum went out onto the balcony. Lately, naturally, he'd gotten thin. He breathed the cool evening air, looking out over République. He'd quit smoking. He unwrapped a stick of mint gum.

"Chewing gum. Check it out, I unwrap it like a condom, it's from doing all those demonstrations. Demonstrations, that's all I ever do."

He put his hands on his hips, a brown shape against the black night as he stood next to the bay window and the green plants.

"To think that there was all that joie de vivre, the community, the sex, the dancing, the politics, and that it left behind such a rotten taste . . . It was as though we'd struck the best deal going. The straights, the leftists, the intellectuals, the women, they were having such a bad time of it. Nothing brought them together, nothing but the famine in Africa and Nelson Mandela. But all we had to do was do what we wanted, what we desired, and it was good, beautiful, and true, all at the same time. When you're defining your own era, you're not aware of it, you think you're building a future. Then one day you realize that this future you're building is just something that people will look back on one day as the past, as something past and gone. That's what it means to live, to live out an era, a time, a moment. All of a sudden—yes—it ends. And it ended badly. Suddenly you start thinking in the middle of fucking, you're thinking and wishing you were fucking, whereas before the two things were one and the same. It was—well, I can't think of a better expression than joie de vivre. Everything my education taught me and my father told me was stupid, vain, shallow, or selfish became, as if by magic, smart, decisive, meaningful, and political. To love a man, to want him, to come inside a man, to make him come. It was crazy. It was better than writing a book, smarter than a book of philosophy, more beautiful than a painting or a symphony, and more meaningful than standing up for the poor. Shit."

He closed the door, and in the living room window I saw myself, amber-colored against the starry sky, sitting cross-legged on the rug, a glass of gin in my hand. I sat there and I listened. There was nobody else around, just us. Neither of us cared much about the next day's column—we knew how to crank it out.

"Want to see what's on TV?"

I turned it on. This is what we'd come to.

6

"In Vienna, in 1872, Dr. Moritz Kaposi diagnosed a certain skin disease, the sarcoma that bears his name. Five mature men were observed to have the condition.

"Ten years later, in Naples, Dr. Amicis described twelve cases.

"Then came the chicken. In 1908 Ellerman and Bang discovered that a filtered extract of leukemia, taken from a chicken they'd used in the experiment, unleashed a cancerous development in the cell.

"Dr. Francis Peyton Rous, in 1911, spoke of a 'retrovirus.'

"It seemed that, thanks to a certain enzyme, the RNA of this virus short-circuited the retranscription of our cells' DNA: the RNA of the virus was an outrageous impostor capable of making us adopt its own signature. And not only did it fool our bodies—it kept fooling them: it mutated.

"He was twenty-five years old, he was a sailor. He died in 1959 in Manchester, with pneumonia, a cytomegaloviral infection, anal fissures, and Kaposi's sarcoma.

"None of this, of course, was widely known. Sometimes things progress in the shadows and the unconscious long before they appear, and their proliferation—sudden, terrible, uncontrollable— is simply the effect, times ten, of what has unfolded powerfully in complete darkness over the preceding years."

So wrote Dominique Rossi and Jean-Philippe Laporte in an issue of *Blason* during the late eighties.

Apart from Dominique, I don't know any survivors from those early years.

"You have to understand, everything had changed. At *Pur Dur*, just before we started *Blason*, I was surrounded by people just like me. Leftists, intellectuals. We wanted to publish Foucault, Fernandez, Duvert, and Sartre, over and over again. And you know, even in '82 or '83, Francis, Jean-Philippe, Jean-Luc couldn't bear to see *Blason* pass on to the next generation. There were more and more ads, everything got much slicker and more commercial, what with the Minitel, but we had no choice. It was new. It was us. The old guard didn't get it. I remember Jean-Luc telling me, when he was dying in the hospital—he was so thin, covered in sores, barely recognizable—'I know you're right, Doumé. I do. But to my mind the whole thing stinks of consumerism, superficiality, Parisianism.' He had a hard time breathing. 'I'd rather just remember.'

"He was thinking of the southwest, where he grew up, the café terraces, the street fights with the radical right, his first love, the FLH, the Front for the Liberation of Homosexuals. He was thinking of that whole underground scene. He'd never been to the States. He didn't want any part of that community. Well— he'd rather just remember.

"'Those first few years we had our fun,' and he told me all over again about the first issues of *Pur Dur* in the seventies, about the smell of leather, about the printers, the subscriptions, the connections with the Trotskyites, and his first love."

Dominique rubbed his upper lip, where his mustache would have been.

"So many of them ended up that way, one after another. It was a massacre. Especially after '87. It was horrifying, right up until about the time I met Will."

He sat up in his wicker chair, mashing down his socks.

"The first time we heard anyone talk about it, seriously I mean, was in 1981, a while after the rumors had started going around in

the States. We were back in France by then. Those were the
glory days of Mitterrand.

"We were in the middle of lunch, Jean-Philippe, Francis,
Jean-Luc, Lionel, and I think two others. I was always the youngest, back then. Then Éric showed up, shaking his head. He'd
just had a big fight with Gilles, a close friend, one of his best
friends, who worked at the Claude Bernard Clinic. According to
Gilles, they were treating a gay flight attendant for a pulmonary
infection, and Gilles, who was in touch with Willy Rozenbaum,
who was assistant director of the clinic, said that there were connections between the infection and this article that had come
out in the MMWR. And then we read it, the MMWR, *Morbidity
and Mortality Weekly Report*. It was the medical bulletin of the
Centers for Disease Control and Prevention in Atlanta. Fuck.
See, I remember the names. I haven't lost everything."

He coughed.

"Of course, we had to teach ourselves medicine—all of it.
Nobody gave a damn about us."

He rubbed his forehead.

"Me, who always flunked biology.

"There was all this talk about a gay cancer, and some people
thought it was linked to poppers. And we certainly did use
poppers.

"Jean-Luc, more than Jean-Philippe, who was deeply skeptical,
wanted us to come up with a response. It was obvious, he thought,
and lots of us agreed, that the whole thing was ideological, it was
political, an excuse to let the cops harass us and close down gay
hangouts. It's martial law, he'd say. They're putting us under
lockdown.

"There was this guy, François, who was president of the Association of Gay Doctors. He ended up writing all these wrong-
headed, backward articles in *Pur Dur* about the disease and how
it was a protofascist creation of the hospital state—but you know

we were all reading Foucault, and this was held up as a kind of evidence, because we were so ghettoized, because we were considered a minority. We didn't believe in random bad luck, and we didn't believe in nature.

"But then nature came back with a vengeance. Nature and the body. It was one thing to talk about the politics of the disease, back when—when I still had my balls, you know. But when you've got the disease, when you're riddled with it, it makes you feel like an envelope, an empty, crumpled-up envelope. When your insides are the enemy, just as much as the outside world, and your own *cells* are letting you down—well, that changes everything. You feel very much in touch with nature, let me tell you, what you feel is that you're dying. I've seen it every time, I've seen it in their eyes. Jean-Philippe beat Jean-Luc to the story, and Francis, who was going off to Mexico, and so we ran an interview with the first patient the clinic lost. Before he died, of course.

"That was in '82. You could feel the pressure building, even in the papers. It had already been two years since Gallo isolated the first human retrovirus, HTLV-1, but we didn't yet have HTLV-3. I read the articles, but what did I know about lymphomas and leucocytes? What struck me, I remember, was how Gallo's oncovirus was supposed to 'immortalize' the target cells, those famous T cells. It immortalized them. I had no idea what this meant, medically, but for a long time I couldn't get the expression out of my head.

"Gilles was the one who got us access to the research. He tried to explain to us about Kaposi's sarcoma, about the pneumocystic pneumonia that was affecting homosexuals. The moment he said 'affecting homosexuals' we'd give him such a hard time. He was always so incredibly patient . . .

"He died in a car crash, in '88. What a sweetheart he was.

"If you kept up the way we did, then you knew by late '81 or early '82 that gays weren't the only ones who got it. People started calling it Acquired Immunodeficiency Syndrome. But where had it come from? From monkeys, for Christ's sake?

"A fifty-nine-year-old father died in Denver. People like Charles Mayaud, Jacques Leibowitch, Odile Picard were all arguing that it had nothing to do with homosexuality; naturally we assumed they'd try to chalk it up to some 'defect,' something in our homosexual DNA, something in our sperm, or blood, or some mineral in our secretions when we fucked. Maybe they'd say it was love itself. The prime mover. *The* thing—*our* thing. We were cursed—and most of us didn't even believe in God. We were cursed, by nothing. By some bodily function, some dysfunction. Next thing you knew, you had the virus, the skin was peeling right off your face.

"So anyway, Gilles put us in touch with the guy in the clinic. Rozenbaum's team told us we shouldn't go see him. These were the guys who founded French Working Group on AIDS, with immunologists, dermatologists, pulmonologists. They kept up with all the latest developments. For reasons of his own, François didn't want us to do it, either. But we jumped on it. We practically had to sneak in to interview the guy at his house, in rue de Clignancourt, in '82.

"What a shock. This was long before AZT or tritherapies. We felt it was going to kill us all, the ground had simply fallen away beneath us. And he was in very bad shape. It was horrible. Even thinking of it makes me sick, even now. We tried to talk to him, he had that look, his eyes dead in the middle of his face— like all the other ones after him. He didn't say much, really, but we understood. He was dead within the year.

"At first it happened more or less at random, you couldn't tell why. Every year, someone else you knew. In '82 alone there were a hundred deaths in the United States. People were looking up the earliest cases, going back to '74. People were talking about Zaire.

"For what, seven, eight years it was part of my life, like a war that starts somewhere at the other end of the world, then spreads to Europe, then suddenly it's happening in your own country. By the end of the eighties, when you and I got to know each other, everyone I used to know was dead. You were just starting then. Jean-Philippe, Jean-Luc, François—like Hervé or Jean-Marie. Everyone. It was winter. They faded away so fast. You noticed the first signs, they developed that look, and you could tell they were taken by surprise, they couldn't hold on, and then what? It was already over. A hospital visit, then the cemetery.

"And the thing is, part of me didn't want to know what was going on. Maybe this was cowardice, partly. I drifted away from the, quote, 'older' men, the guys who weren't my own age. I got to know the younger generation. I went out. I stopped going to funerals for the old gang, the guys from the seventies, the militants. I felt very guilty about it. But, for a few years, while the disease kept spreading, I can say that at least I had moments of that same joie de vivre. While the disease was spreading around me, I sought out the bright lights. I have no regrets on that score. I'm glad to have had those moments of light.

"Obviously, the memory stays with you. You simply live with it. Nowadays there's a new generation with its own codes, its own behavior, and someone like—well, you know. I'd rather remember. I'd rather set my memories in order."

He tasted his cider.

He smiled.

"Those first few years, though, they spoiled me."

7

In 1986 or '87 Doum founded an association of gay activists, on the American model. The idea was to support people with HIV and, at the same time, to challenge the power structures—structures *plural*, as Foucault said, Foucault who himself had recently died—and to defend gays, lesbians, and all the "factions" that were starting to spring up: queer, transgender, and the rest of it.

Three people helped him set up Stand (or as it was originally known, Stand-UP: Section Transgenre d'Attaque de la Norme et de Défense de l'Union Pédé). There was Éric, an artist and writer involved with theater; Rico, a salesman with connections in advertising; and Philippe, a fixture in his overcoat, almost a sort of elder statesman, a former Surrealist, a photography buff, a man of leisure, a Proustian, who lent them his apartment near Rambuteau.

What started it all was this bitter argument Doum had with that old Party hack Daniel. Doum had gone to get the Party's backing. Daniel, who found himself in the opposition and had lost his post as a deputy (he'd taken a cover job in real estate), was trying to mobilize the Socialists around a Rocardian reform—whatever that was, something politically important at the time that no one remembers now. "Sure I'd love to help," he told Doumé, "but what have you got in mind? Who or what are we protesting? Nature? What do you want the left to do about it?

We're talking about a disease. That's what science is for." Doum just stood there, openmouthed. He was shattered.

He talked to Philippe about it. It was true, there was nothing to be done.

And then Rico decided they should at least have a rally, in front of the headquarters of the Socialists, who were no longer in power. Doum made an antispeech. They all covered their mouths with big strips of black tape and lay down, playing dead, in the street.

They'd hung up just one sign: "The dead don't speak. We have nothing to say."

Of course, they'd been inspired by American activists. They were sick of traditional demonstrations. Those had become predictable, in an age when what everyone wanted was something new, an event. They didn't just attack the establishment, they went after "civil society," as people were starting to call it. There weren't many of them, but that was almost better for the media. The TV crews showed up.

Daniel, on his way out of the building, shook his head, refusing to talk to the cameras: "It's the end of politics, it's pure spectacle. Excuse me."

Doum always had a temper, and now he was furious. "For fuck's sake," he told Philippe, "now Dany's giving us lectures?" Dany the operator, the strategist who kept a maze in his head, whose ideals had all vanished into the space behind his eyes and left only the sensation of power anchored in his guts, in his growing belly.

Doum tore off his strip of gaffer tape. He had no megaphone, no banners. This wasn't the old kind of demonstration, far from it. He got up, he walked over to the cameras, and he said:

"We have nothing to say and they censure us. We're supposed to just sit there and let *them* tell us what to do—the Party, the state, Papa, and all those paternalistic institutions.

"So—what do we faggots want? I'll tell you what we want, we

want to live. And what do you want? I'll tell you, you want all of us faggots dead, you want there to be no more faggots, you want us wiped out, you want even the word and the reality of it to disappear. You tell us to wait like good little boys, to be careful and responsible. You tell us that if we die, we're a little bit to blame. But tell me, just who are you? Are you the Church, to tell us that we're sinners? Are you the state, to tell us to be responsible?

"No, we say, it's not right. We're not going to just disappear. Science won't be coming to our rescue out of the generosity of its heart, will it? No! We have to pressure the pharmaceutical companies, we have to pressure the politicians, night and day—let them feel the pressure we're under! Yes! We have to break the silence and stand! Stand up! We have to act! We have to push back! We have to wake up the world."

He stopped to take a breath, his hair short and bleached, and he pointed his finger right in the middle of the screen. "And if I'm guilty of being sick, you're the ones who are responsible. We have the right to love, and you have the duty to save us."

There it was. Five years later it was part of the culture. AIDS was there, so was Stand. People died, people protested, people protected themselves, people gave money, people did research. It was part of life, part of the era, part of the whole.

ENCOUNTERS

8

For a year Willie lived on the streets, near the Gare du Nord, and in squats where crackheads lived. He'd learned to spit on the system.

He became a type. First he shaved off his hair, and started to hold his head up; he had a strong chest, beautifully defined. He'd call himself an artist, meaning an outlaw. He'd say he was writing some *piece*, he'd say he had works in progress, shit going on. A kind of installation, like the performance artists he came across in squats. My guess is he wanted to shout words while some rockers did their thing. But there were no rockers anymore.

He was living out a mythology he never quite got the hang of. He wanted tattoos, a band, a look, like those pictures of James Dean or Tupac that are sold illegally in the metro. He liked those. No one knew much about him. In real life he was all alone. He always said the opposite, of course. He never went out with anyone. He had this rehearsal space where they let him crash, he had his blanket. He'd have liked to own a pet rat, but he never found one. He stuck to northern Paris. "'S all good," he'd say, "'s all good. I've got shit in the works." Even the lingo he used was borrowed. He drank beer. It was obvious he didn't like beer. He was surrounded by bums. Washed-up punks, a couple of baseheads, nobody friendly. He was a nice kid, shy, he scratched his head, he shaved when he could. He panhandled.

Later he became a somebody, but he was nobody then. I don't think he even realized that things weren't working out. He clung to this idea that he had friends, that he had a project, none of which was true. He came from the provinces, he wasn't a musician, he wasn't a writer, he wasn't anything. With his face he might have been a model. He had this way of looking down and scratching his head. I knew Pierre, who knew the guy who ran this bar, who knew people at the rehearsal space. I was looking to do a profile, something original, for the little paper, something about a guy living on the margins who was slightly ridiculous.

He's the one who told me: "There's this weird dude, a homeless guy, who writes this completely impenetrable shit, he's always reading it at you, he has all these theories, he drives everyone totally fucking insane at the bar on a more or less regular basis. It could be something for the magazine. The kid's a piece of work."

The magazine in question was a pretentious piece of shit. Its sole mission was making fun of people. We wrote about Paris trends. It was for students who believed in the "avant-garde" and thought they were a beacon for the masses. I was in the middle of extricating myself. Dominique, whom I'd met thanks to Leibowitz, had held out the chance of a job at *Libération*. I wasn't about to say no.

I said yes. The point is I was getting out. It was my last "UFO Profile," about nightlife, two columns on the next-to-last page.

He stammered and he smelled. He had trouble stringing a sentence together. If you looked at him from the side he was beautiful. I said, "Are you Willie?" He didn't say yes. I turned off the tape. We were at a concert on a barge, down on the quais. It was clear, actually, that he was beautiful, that he didn't belong there. You could tell from the way he sat on his stool, perched with half his ass over the void.

I bought him a beer. He was badly dressed, to put it mildly. He was ill at ease and out of shape.

He babbled for a while. None of what he said made any sense. None of it. He was indignant and he didn't even know it. There was nothing political, nothing artistic about anything he said. He wasn't cultured. It was all just a mishmash. He was young, I guessed he wasn't even twenty.

I was the one who put it to him, just like that: "Why aren't you gay?" It struck me as a kind of truth.

I couldn't take him to bed, which had been my first thought. It took me only two or three minutes to figure that out. He didn't understand. He said, "I'm not. I'm not."

Well. I put my arm around his shoulder. "What are you, then?" I said. I was twenty. I felt twenty years older than him. I was freelancing for *Libération*, I was practically on the payroll, I was seeing someone, I'd done my internship for Sciences-Po. Careerwise, I was set.

I had the apartment near Bastille. It's not as if we went out together, but I helped him. He moved in with me, he stayed one week, then he stayed another.

We used to laugh a lot, back then. You wouldn't have guessed it, but Willie had his own very particular sense of fun. I'd dress him up in my evening clothes. He was very hairy. When I asked him whether that embarrassed him, he ran out and got himself waxed—and stayed waxed most of the time. He loved wigs, he loved jewelry. I remember seeing him in drag for the first time while I lay on the cherry-colored sofa. He was such a terrible actor. It's hard to believe how stiff, how uptight he was back then, if you knew him later on. Clearly, something was holding him back.

He was pretty once he shaved a little, put on some perfume, one or two pieces of jewelry and a T-shirt that actually fit. I whistled, he looked so damn good. I slept in his arms, that time. He just lay there rigid.

He lived completely in the past. He was the kind of guy who loved poetry, who wrote poetry, like Verlaine, like Rimbaud. He listened to rock, he talked about punks. It had all happened before his time. He was a prude, everything in him was so tightly coiled. He'd have hated disco because it would have struck him as indecent, as dirty. I loved to tease him. I had no shame. I walked around the apartment naked. I talked to him about Leibowitz. I explained that I was afraid of hurting Leibowitz because he was so sensitive. That I respected him, that I didn't want to fuck up my relationship with him . . . When it came to him I was just as prudish and all the rest of it as Willie. What can I say? It was the early nineties.

He'd listen and, as usual back then, he wouldn't say anything. Just sit there, arms resting on his knees. He'd start talking all at once, and he talked in a very vague, abstract way, as if he wanted to say something true—he never did, obviously. He never talked about his past. He'd conjure up a very vague, semi-messianic future. None of it made a hell of a lot of sense.

When I got him drunk, he'd scratch his balls, he'd laugh, drily, and he'd do a striptease. He'd put on my scarves, my lingerie, my rings and necklaces. And what do you know? It worked.

When he woke up the next day, he'd cough a bit, he wouldn't take an aspirin or anything back then. He read *philosophy*.

I listened to him. He had a way of making even the simplest ideas sound complicated. He wasn't Leibowitz. He didn't understand the first thing about ideas or their meaning. But he already had a knack for living, even in the midst of all his bullshit, that Leibowitz never had.

Not long afterward, maybe a few days later, on a Saturday, I took him for a night out, more or less as a friend. That's when he first saw Doumé. It wasn't something expected or planned, it was a sort of statistical inevitability. Doumé had become the prince of the night, back then. He'd gone out with Jimmy Somerville, he was known for his sexual prowess, but this was the transitional phase when all that joie de vivre started to seem a little sad. William was such a contrast. The kid never really fit in. In a way, I think, that's what touched Doumé and did him in.

9

I woke him up, I shook him, I told him: "I have to go do a profile. Feel like coming with me? Want to get out of the house and meet somebody?"

Will never really had a say, he just followed.

Dominique was coming to pick me up in his car, we were going to do a piece on a restaurateur, a famous chef with two Michelin stars who was about to open a "People's Canteen" in a couple of different places, a concept designed for workers and everybody else who didn't make enough to go out for haute cuisine. The idea was to take *grands plats* and sell them on the cheap. That's what *Libé* had come to—profiling the likes of him.

Doum was, as always, in shirtsleeves and dark glasses. He drove an old Dauphine he took good care of. He had style.

"Hey there . . . Liz?"

He glanced at Willie, standing behind me with his hands in his pockets. The sun was out.

"Is that him?"

I discreetly told him yes.

"Hello, William, pleased to meet you."

Willie stretched out his hand. Doum had quite a handshake.

"OK, we're headed for the Chevreuse Valley, that's where Gériolles lives—promising, no?"

William, sitting in back, with his seatbelt on, asked what he meant.

Doum-Doum checked him out in the rearview mirror, chewing his gum: "Well, anyone who lives in the Chevreuse Valley is doing pretty well."

"Oh yeah, right."

We drove along. Doum turned up the music.

"What's that?"

"Paul Oakenfold, a special mix, the next one's Mike Pickering, a personal selection from the Hacienda."

"What kind of music is it?"

Willie kept sitting up straight in the backseat.

"Euro house. *Ecstasy, baby!* The music of tomorrow. If you like it, the future's yours. Otherwise you're yesterday."

"Oh."

He was playing this on a ghetto blaster he kept on the dashboard in front of the passenger seat. More or less in my lap. I tried to make conversation. Doum kept looking past me, behind his dark glasses, toward the back.

William was looking for something to say, but he kept his mouth shut.

"Well, here we are."

We waited ten minutes at the gate, surrounded by hedges and thickets growing along a comfortable old stone wall.

Gériolles was, naturally, an utter moron. We asked him the standard questions about his childhood, he went off on long, tear-jerking monologues about his parents, his childhood, and him, him, him, his humble background, how much his roots meant to him, and all the specifics reeked of self-promotion. The stuff you'd learn in your first three marketing classes. I sat taking notes. He talked a lot about people who talked about him. We did a lot of smiling and nodding.

He figured he'd make margin on the presentation, decor, tableware, and staff. These were the years when journalistic interviews started to look like press releases. You had a mounting sense, without its quite yet feeling normal, that you were talking to a product, to something recorded and memorized. Only the lips were still moving. Right away we realized that the whole point of the thing was to establish some stupid brand, some line of products with his name on them, which would end up in supermarkets, in the prepared-food aisle.

Will asked to use the toilet. We'd introduced him as our assistant, he was the one who held the tape recorder. It wasn't that I was ashamed of him, but still.

When he came back twenty minutes later, smiling as if he'd just taken an enormous dump, I shot him a black look—and we got up to leave.

Gériolles shook hands with each of us, beaming and thanking us for our attention—for a second I was worried, because Willie wasn't exactly a stickler for personal hygiene. Gériolles invited us to the opening of his canteen, he even said he was eager to hear what we thought of it.

As a journalist you learn that these are the kind of people who always get ahead. Which means you have a choice. Either you say to yourself that getting ahead isn't worth it, or else you decide you'd better admire these people and imitate them as best you can.

Opening the back door, Will snickered. It was chilly out, and he looked rosy-cheeked with the petunias behind him, his feet crunching on the gray gravel. Out of his pocket he took a kind of statuette, laughing, and it shone in the light—a golden toque.

"What the fuck? Will—what the fuck is that?"

He looked down at the ground. "The guy's an asshole, isn't he?"

I was ashen. He'd stolen the fucker's trophy. I let him have it—I could have exploded, I was so angry. "Jesus Christ, Will, you don't get it, if this guy figures out that you, that we . . . He's a fucking big deal . . . and I just started at the paper . . ."

Doum had taken off his dark glasses, he was shaking with

laughter. "It's OK," he said, "don't worry." He put his hand on Will's shoulder, like a father.

"All right, you know what we're going to do?"

Will shrugged.

"We're going to give the dipshit back his thing."

I couldn't believe my eyes. Will trusted him. Doum rang the bell. Gériolles appeared, all smiles.

"I beg your pardon, you must have left this in the garden. But you ought to be careful. It'll rust. Underneath the gold plating it must be really cheap, and if it rains . . . well. See you around."

Gériolles stammered.

"Uh, thanks, thanks again . . ."

As he shut the car door Will gave Doum a puzzled look. Doum started the car.

"Don't sweat it, William. You'll learn. We're going to fuck him. But not by stealing his gold-plated trophies. That's for losers. Pull a stunt like that and you wind up in jail."

He adjusted the rearview mirror.

"No, no. You have to use your words. We're going to murder him in print, in the article. We'll make people laugh. That's what kills. That's what gets them where they live. You have to use language, education . . ."

He tapped his skull.

"Use your head, William."

He drove off toward Paris.

"That's how you cut somebody down. You have to learn, William, you have to be smarter than that. Look, I feel like kicking his ass too. I just know how to go about it, that's all."

William was wide-eyed, slumped.

Then a moment passed and Doum added, as an afterthought, "Come by my place tonight, I'll show you how it's done."

10

Leibowitz became famous, in the mid-eighties, thanks to a book that had nothing to do with his reflections on politics, at least not in any obvious way. It was a book about love.

Even President Mitterrand had read *Fidelity for Life: On Promise-Keeping and Our Time*. He mentioned it in a conversation with Jean Lacouture, and Robert Badinter reported the anecdote. The president is supposed to have said, "If he'd seen any action in Cambodia or Afghanistan, you know, if he'd lived a little, I'd have made him my Malraux."

Well. Leibowitz looked good on TV. Back then he still had his hair. Hair matters, on TV.

I read it over and over again. As I remember, its gist was that modern times have made a cult of the casual relationship, of the freedom to choose one's partners, of rejecting what really matters, and we all subscribe to this cult, we've all forgotten what it means to promise. When you promise, you commit yourself to the future, the future of your whole life, in that one single moment. And Leibowitz said that time, true time, doesn't consist of a series of moments when you think, I love, now I don't love, now I love. True time is the duration of a promise. When you love, you commit yourself to loving even when the feeling has passed. You do it out of respect for your old intention to love the other person forever. And that sort of time, the promised time, was the only defense against time as we commonly know it, sliced and diced by consumer culture into little snippets of fake freedom. The only defense against individualism, against the civilization of the now, against the hedonism of today. Of course, that didn't mean people shouldn't get divorced or have affairs, no, only that we had to get back to the idea of enduring love, of the enduring promise, and of fidelity in its truest sense: being faithful to something that may, perhaps, be in the past. Faithful even though it's in the past—faithful *because* it's in the past. The book was short, and it was full of quotations from Husserl, Levinas, Ricoeur, Kundera, even Derrida. It was acclaimed for its erudition, plus lots of people went out and bought it. It was definitely the perfect gift if you were shopping for a girl.

After I found out at Sciences-Po that I was going to have Leibowitz as a professor, I used to walk around with the book in my pocket. I took it everywhere.

After that I never looked at it again.

The night when he invited me to the restaurant, he already had less hair. I mean compared to on TV. He told me, looking down at his wineglass, "You know . . ."

I'd just finished telling him about the book—how I always carried it with me.

He pinched the bridge of his nose very hard, the way he always does when he's about to cry, and he told me: "You know, that book, this is terrible, but I don't believe in it anymore." It was the thing that had made him famous.

He was sobbing.

"It's got my name on the cover, but I wouldn't write a word of it now."

I consoled him, I took him in my arms, for the first time.

And afterward . . .

Well, it's sitting there on my shelf.

11

This is the one thing that I never actually witnessed, the one thing in this whole story.

They were together for five years, roughly. I saw them socially, of course. All I can describe is what I glimpsed, that and a little bit more. But I began to see less and less of them, there's that, too. The gay community was exploding and, at the same time, retreating into itself.

They went out, they had connections, Le Dépôt didn't yet exist. Everyone joked about their being a couple, but there was no getting around it. Doum punched a guy because he wouldn't stop hitting on Willie. By now Willie had become very beautiful, he'd gained confidence, he had poise, he'd started working out.

Those days, the early nineties, saw the rise of Gay Pride. You heard more and more about the cause of gay rights. Doum was a constant presence on TV. He was the public face of Stand, he ran *Blason*, and now you could get it on the newsstands. It wasn't really underground anymore.

They had an apartment near Saint-Paul. They had a good life. Their place was a nerve center. I hung out there when I could, though I was spending lots of time with the Leib in those days. There was the nightlife, there were the parties—but the recognition of gay rights and freedom didn't come out of nowhere.

It was a kind of flip side, a sign of cultural compassion, and the price was AIDS.

In three years Doum had lost a dozen friends from the eighties. Rico, Éric, Pascal—they had died very quickly. The photographer, Francis, who had meant so much to him—he told Doum not to come to the hospital and see him, at the end.

William, I think, didn't quite understand. Or maybe he understood better than Doumé. Maybe he understood too well. Which is to say he was younger, he hadn't come into contact with that generation, except through Doumé, and he felt bad for him, but he would have liked to live through what they had lived through. He'd have liked to experience that joie de vivre. More and more, meetings took the place of parties and sex in Doum's life. Stand took priority, whatever else they were doing, and it took time. Willie helped, a lot I think, putting everything together, while Stand rose from the ashes of the dead.

He loved Doumé.

Nobody died of joie de vivre, they died of the disease, but the disease cast its shadow between the joy they'd known and death, between the joy and the legacy of those corpses. "And the disease had become the grand faggot passion," as Will would write a few years later. "The disease was the new Look." Doumé's face grew strained, and when he coughed, you found yourself looking away. Will followed wherever he went.

In their personal lives, they were characters. You never saw one without the other. William was speaking better, it's true. He spoke up, and he laughed. These were things he learned from Doumé. It was always Doumé who put his hand on Willie's shoulder. All Willie did was learn.

Once they took a trip. They went to Venice. Doum joked about it at the office. They went over Christmas. It was such a couple thing to do—such a *straight* thing to do. Venice . . . but so what, it was beautiful.

Plus they were always going back and forth to New York. Doum wasn't extravagant, but he'd always had money. He simply took money for granted. So many things were a discovery to Willie, practically everything in fact.

He had two piercings.

I can see them making out on my sofa on Willie's birthday. Doum gave him two plants, wrapped up in silver paper, and Nan Goldin's book. Doum got Willie to read Foucault, and Doum knew Foucault so well—I mean personally, plus he took his courses at the Collège de France—that he never really bothered with the books. Willie was reading everything that Doum knew without having to read it, without even having to think of it anymore. He'd read ten, maybe twenty times, what Foucault said about the war—thanks to Dominique, who was a close friend of Defert's, he had access to students' notes, to the archives, to the unpublished *Aveux de la chair*.

One night we were dancing and I saw them and got it. I mean, I saw them sexually. Doum was the more sexual one, at the time, though Will said he stopped getting hard-ons later on. That all he thought about was AIDS.

Doum knew he was positive long before he met Will. I don't even know whether Will knew what that entailed, back then, back in the beginning.

I remember bringing them breakfast in bed. They'd be like, "Thanks, 'bye." I was alone, while Leibo was off skiing with his wife and children. They'd put me to bed and we'd watch TV together. It seemed as though I was always sadder than they were. I'd hurry out of the apartment so they could be by themselves; I'd wolf down a pancake with maple syrup. Domi loved to make pancakes. I'd go through their pockets. Back then they used to hide their condoms.

I was rather lonely.

Doumé used to tell Will, gently stroking his neck, "We're happy, isn't it dumb, and we don't even have to try."

He kept writing articles for *Libé*, but from then on his real life was Stand. I took his place at the culture desk. I wrote a little bit about everything, I worked a lot.

I don't know just how they were happy, that's precisely the kind of private thing that, when you see it from outside, ceases to be what it is—when you talk about it and when you write it down.

TAKING SIDES

12

Doum got Willie a job.

He was going to write a column for *Blason*; whatever he wanted, it was up to him. Doum read them over, Doum corrected them.

It occurs to me that this must have been William's first job since he quit business school in Amiens. (Which was something he never talked about.)

So anyway, we were celebrating.

Their place was very much the way you'd imagine it, very typical of those years. Next to the tacky sixties bookshelf, the fake Lava Lamp, and on the beige ottoman, around the designer coffee table, between the lamps, all these sweet little lanterns, very chic. Doum was the one who did the cooking, Doum was the one who brought the chicken to the table. And Willie sat waiting.

We had chicken in spicy chocolate sauce, à la Oaxaca. Willie grabbed the carving knife and, as he picked his front tooth with a fingernail, he cut off a drumstick and served himself first, as if it were the most natural thing in the world.

I remember Doum brushing his mustache with his thumb and taking off his apron. He'd barely turned around.

"Why did you help yourself? What about us?"

Willie's mouth fell open, he was completely surprised, he gave Doum a puzzled look and spread his arms.

"Well, I mean, you know . . ."

He was having fun with it.

"No, in fact, I don't know. That's not the way you do it. First you serve everybody else, then you put things on your plate. That's how it's done. Didn't your father ever teach you that?"

"My pff . . . pff . . . pff . . ." Little flecks of saliva flew from his lips. "My father, whatever. I took the thigh so I could give you the good part."

I was smoking, I kept smoking. I drew the ashtray closer.

"The good part? Of the chicken? You mean the breast?"

"That's what I said—the good part."

Doumé coughed, his awful wet cough that I couldn't help hating.

"The good part? Where on earth did you get that from?"

Willie lay back on the sofa, showing off his sculpted body. He purposely thrust his hips forward like he was telling Doumé to shut up and fuck him, he knew perfectly well which was the good part.

"No, no. Listen, if you want to know which part is 'good,' you ask me which part I prefer, and then that's the part you give me. But you ask."

"But everyone knows the breast—"

"No, maybe your parents told you the breast was the good part, because they were buying frozen turkey parts on sale. But there is no good part, Will, there's just the part I like, that's why you ask me and wait to serve yourself. That's all, it isn't rocket science."

"You're being a dick."

Will switched plates with him. He was acting like a teenager. He had a ring in his nose and close-cropped hair, dyed blond.

Doum sighed. I laughed.

"I don't like the drumstick, sweetheart. I like the breast."
"Oh," Will said, "so how come you're being such a jerk?"
"Because I don't like it when you serve yourself first."
He patted him on the thigh, we ate.
Six months later they'd broken up.

13

During the nineties, Leib's parents lived in Maisons-Alfort, not far from the train station. It was nicer than anywhere they'd ever lived, which wasn't saying much.

Leib talked about them constantly. And I mean nonstop.

Oh, but it's not as if he wasn't interested in mine—in my parents, I mean. He was always asking after my father. He just had an inordinate interest in parents, in general. It was one of the first things he wanted to know about people. Their parents. After all, wasn't that where they came from?

Obviously I'd never met his, he'd never met mine. Except once, when I went to pick him up at the Maisons-Alfort station, at the end of one of his parental visits. All I'd ever seen of Maisons-Alfort was hotels, or really just the one hotel. I was extremely familiar with the hotel. Anyway, for whatever reason, he brought his parents and introduced me.

I was his student, though I was a little old to be a student. He referred to me as a graduate researcher.

The thing was, he simply couldn't stand for you not to know his parents. His father was an auto worker, as humble as could be, a Polish Jew. He'd spent a year in Auschwitz, almost to the day, I think. Leibowitz got someone to publish his account of life in the camps.

He never said "Papa," he said "my father," and this embarrassed his father. I could see that right away.

I spent half an hour at their house. It was pretty grim, and Leibowitz never stopped railing at them for not doing anything.

He'd always go on about it, after we made love. "I booked them a trip to Venice, and they did it again, they bailed out, they said they were fine where they were."

His father couldn't drive anymore, and they didn't have any friends or other family. Leibowitz did everything for them. They'd smile, more and more distantly, they'd say yes—and then they wouldn't do it, whatever it was. His father would always just say the same thing, patting Leibo on the shoulder, "Jean-Michel, haven't we earned a little rest? Tell me, am I wrong?" And he'd smile.

They were proud of him.

And he was proud of them, too, but it made him suffer. They thought of him as happy, and that was what made them proudest. His father was always telling the same stories about the camps and, I know for a fact, it drove Leibo up the wall. But he felt bad that it bored him shitless, sitting there while his father told the same old story about the guard over a glass of wine, the same story he'd heard since he was seven. He told me, "When I was little I'd never listen to what he said, but I learned everything from him. Now I always listen and there's nothing for me to learn."

Leibo did all he could. He had written for them, he'd written about them. He pulled strings for his father to get a medal. He took his mother to buy groceries. And just look at them.

"Well, son, what can I tell you? Sometimes it's over before it's over . . ."

His mother made the soup, always the same soup. He bought foie gras, they didn't like it. They weren't observant. His father had never been political, ever. They loved France, and Leibo used to bawl them out, when he was a kid, because he couldn't understand their patriotism and their distrust of communism. He resented them, in those days, for never having got an education.

They didn't understand.

They didn't understand that France had helped deport the Jews, they wouldn't even hear about it, or about how they'd been exploited as members of the working class (back then, Leibowitz considered his wife a "worker" because she did the housework).

His father never had much to say to these arguments, they didn't even seem to annoy him.

"Oh, Jean-Michel . . . that's life, you know."

Later on, Jean-Michel never stopped praising his parents for not having an education and yet understanding everything. He came to recognize that he himself had been given a scholarship, that the Republic had granted him the education his father never had—and that his father was a republican for that very reason. By the time we were together Leibowitz had become a republican, an anticommunist, and a patriot. It almost made him cry when he thought about the small but glorious wages that they'd been so proud to contribute to his education—and now here he was, making real money, thanks to that.

He told his father, when I was there, "Father, you're absolutely right."

And his father answered, "Oh, Jean-Michel, that's life, isn't it."

He'd never had an education, it was as simple as that.

One day Dominique told me, "You know, Leibowitz's problem is that he always feels persecuted because he wishes he were like his father, and his father's not like him."

I laughed.

"For an analyst, you come pretty cheap."

"Oh, Liz, analysis doesn't exist."

But Leibowitz put it the exact same way: "What's sad about parents is that one is like them, but one is *not* them."

I stroked his chest, in the hotel, and I gently said, "Dominique says the same."

"No, it's different for him. He's gay."

"So?"

"So he's bound to hate psychoanalysis. He can't understand. He doesn't believe in his father—he can't want to be like him."

"Ah."

14

In the late nineties Leibowitz made his headquarters at the Bouillon Racine, a restaurant in the Fifth Arrondissement, on boulevard Saint-Michel. He was teaching at Sciences-Po, near boulevard Raspail, but he liked to eat in the neighborhood of the Sorbonne, where he'd studied and where he still held regular seminars and lectures.

Students were always coming up to the Leib. They wore long coats. They carried leather satchels. They had floppy hair and gloves and would gesture a lot with their hands, trying to seem ten years older than they were. Their deference, formality, and earnestness used to drive Doumé up the wall. There he'd sit in the booth, waiting for their conversation to end, counting the little colored tiles on the floor.

"I beg your pardon, Rossi."

Leibowitz was in his element, talking a mile a minute, pushing back what was left of his hair, letting his sautéed scallops get cold.

With his well-polished pointy shoes, he'd tap his foot and argue until he'd taken the student's measure: like any good strategist, he always looked out for his most faithful disciples. His old students remembered the favor: as doctors, professors, journalists, executives, bankers, diplomats, or prefects they all stayed in touch and, most often, on good terms.

"I'm sorry, Rossi, where were we? Oh yes—Miller."

Leibowitz poked at his food. He'd held on to the old *lycée* habit of calling his intimates by their last names.

They had lunch once a month. Dominique, in his tracksuit, with his carefully tended goatee, had the always slightly bitter feeling of no longer belonging to this world of academic institutions, which he'd left early to join the community. He dabbed the corners of his mouth with a checkered napkin, sighed, and went back to his point: "William, my God. You can't imagine what he's like. He's still just a kid. He's like, well, he's like Rimbaud or something. He's out of control. And I just can't keep up anymore. It tires me out. You understand, I need to take care of myself now."

He swallowed some pills. He'd started taking tranquilizers.

Leibowitz chewed on his lettuce.

"The trouble is you forgive him, Rossi. You can't forgive everything. I do it too, you know, it's a habit with all of us on the left. We're always forgiving toward people we think of as oppressed, you know? Meanwhile he acts like a thug. Don't take this the wrong way, but you need to wake up. That boy is unhinged, and one of these days he's going to hurt you."

Doum smiled and picked his front teeth.

"Oh, but I like thugs. Didn't you know? He makes me face my own contradictions. I just feel a little bit old for it, that's all I'm saying."

Leibowitz sniffed and sopped his bread through the last of his julienne.

"I'm telling you, he's an operator. You have to protect yourself."

"Protect myself?" Doum laughed through his wet cough.

"A little pervert like that . . ."

He stopped. Doum had flushed red.

"Take that back."

"Listen, Dominique. If I—"

"You know what that is, Jean-Michel? It's homophobia, pure and simple. You really crossed the line, and I—I can't stand it anymore—"

"Rossi, come on . . . calm down. I wasn't trying to make any generalizations. It's just that—well, you're not together anymore. I only meant he's a bum. He's a loser."

"You've really turned into a shit, Jean-Michel, with all your hypocrisy. You've turned into a bastard. Spouting this faggot-bashing bullshit . . . Every time you open your mouth you go further and further to the right, as if, as if—you've turned into a homophobe yourself. And when you say a thing like that, you're insulting *me*."

"Please, take it easy! Listen, I'm sorry if I said anything—"

"Sorry won't cut it. Not this time. I'm sick of it, Jean-Michel."

Doum got up, his face red and swollen, knocking over a chair. He left his medicine on the table. He was stammering. "I am sick and tired of guys who think it's fine to go and sleep with some girl as if it were nothing, and then hold forth to their students—"

He went on to say something about "heterofascists," according to Jean-Michel. Dominique always swore to me, albeit somewhat perfunctorily, that he never said any such thing.

In his shock Jean-Michel shouted out, "Don't you talk that way about . . . about my parents!"

Jean-Michel didn't understand. He talked to me about it. It wounded him deeply.

It was the first time I heard him say, "The gays are contaminated by their political rhetoric, even when it comes to personal relations. It's like a kind of disease. Yes, a disease. You see, it's a symptom of our era. What's clear is that it has become impossible, nowadays, to have a *healthy* relationship with a homosexual."

There was so much hurt in his face (that's how I took it) that I kissed him.

He started saying the same thing more often, in a more developed way—then he wrote a piece about it. And I know, I just know, that was the day it began.

15

He cut off the radio.

"I can't stand that atrocious stuff, that noise pollution."

I was getting out of the shower.

"It's called house. It's the kind of music Dominique and Will listen to. It's music for dancing to, that's all."

"Music? How can you say that? They force it on us, day in and day out, it's become the official music, the Muzak. If I don't feel like dancing, I'm not going to dance. That's my right. The entire world isn't some kind of giant dance club. And what's worst is that they refer to it as music. 'Music.' Words lose their meaning if you use them any which way. And all of these magazines, all of this obsession with newness, as if newness had some special claim to truth . . . The sound of tomorrow—ugh."

I just said yes. He wasn't completely wrong, he knew that I was a part of all that—and I didn't really put up an argument.

"It's not that it's sheer pop, that it's rhythmically and melodically uninteresting, that it's completely bound to the same old structures, the same old three chords—no, that's not what bothers me. What bugs me is that this stuff passes for sophistication, for artistry, a masterpiece of the human spirit, as if it were just as good as, say, Haydn or Britten, all because it's clever, because it has a hook, because something about it *sells*. We're losing all sense of value, of what makes a real work of art. When I see people on the left, intelligent, cultured people, like Dominique, at his age, who pretend to like that stuff, who force you to pay tribute to the latest thing because it's alive, it's young, it's 'new,' it's the Mozart of today. Well, that's just crap."

"He's not pretending."

"Of course he is. He's hiding from himself. I knew him when he was eighteen. He loved Shostakovich."

I slipped into my nightgown.

"It's decadence, plain and simple, Liz. You can't pretend that stuff is somehow 'progressive' just because some minority latches onto it, or because it's somehow of the people, because it's popular. Is that a reactionary thing to say? No. Really, it's become intolerable. They tell us to shut up, they tell us we're not supposed to say anything, that we can't call shit shit, that we can't point out that shit is different from art. We're supposed to tolerate everything. Look at how the homosexual community—for good reason, it's their right—look at how they impose their norms on everyone else, by default. Look at the way men are pictured in advertisements, the muscles, the fitness, and that music, everywhere, look at how they've changed the connection that we have to our own sexuality. Even women . . ."

Precisely . . .

(He wasn't listening.)

"It started as a statement. But it's become the mainstream. We're all supposed to conform to homosexual standards of beauty, the biceps, the tight T-shirts, putting on makeup, wearing tank tops, and all this sex-machine music . . ."

Precisely . . .

"You know, Liz, I'm actually in the middle of a piece about decadence, somebody needs to take a stand, to take a step back. They let themselves get caught up in the spirit of the era—we all do—and it's all a complete fantasy, the Internet, telecommunication, all of this fleeting lust . . . We have to learn how to *think* again."

All right . . .

"It's a statement of resistance. At the end of the day it's a question of ideology, and . . . Jesus, you're beautiful."

"Thank you."

I let down my hair.

He let go of me.

"I'm sorry, I can't. It's just . . ."

I sighed and sat up.

"Is it Sara?"

"It's not just that, it's this whole era, all this sex for sale, plastered up everywhere, in the music. It's become impossible to have any kind of intimate love, any kind of actual desire . . ."

I stretched out next to him, frowning.

"You know, it's much nicer like this. You know, it's almost an act of resistance just to know, still, how to hold hands."

After a second, I couldn't help smiling All right: I took his hand.

How could I keep from looking down there? I giggled.

"What's the matter, Liz?"

"Nothing. It's just that, all this stuff about decadence, it seems like you're really taking it to heart."

And I slipped my hand around his dick.

He was annoyed at first, then he decided to play along.

"You're the worst, Liz. Look at this. What is the world coming to?"

And we both burst out laughing.

THE GLORY
OF MEN

16

That night Will had a toothache. He took two aspirin, he held his jaw, and he explained: "It's my motherfucking wisdom tooth. See, Liz, my incisors are too big and so, oh *fuck*, the tooth is pushing up behind them, and so it's pushing on all the other teeth, and so there my tooth, not that one, the one right in front of that one, it's like they're pushing it *out*, and so the thing is, yes, of course it fucking hurts, I have to keep my fingernail stuck between my teeth, like that, to sort of push back on them, but then it keeps bleeding all over my hand."

"Why don't you have them pull it?"

He had this dumb giggle.

"Pull it!"

"Well, why not?"

"Please. Have them pull out my own tooth? Why not my left testicle?"

Those were the days when he favored a violet scarf and lots of pink satin.

On our way out we bumped into Lilian.

"Hey, Will! How's it going?"

"It's cool. Have you read Bret Easton Ellis?"

"Huh? I mean, yeah. Yeah, yeah. I mean, why do you ask?"

"You think he's cool? You like him? You like his stuff?"

"Totally! I totally do like his stuff! You, Will, you like him too?"

"I hate it. I fucking hate it. I mean, people who like it, I hate them. I hate people who like Bret Easton Ellis. Do you hear me? I'm talking to you."

"Um, yeah, I mean yeah, but—"

"So why don't you go fuck yourself."

I asked, "What did Lilian do to you?"

"You didn't see what was going on? Oh, Liz—OK, so that little faggot knows I worship Ellis, I mean he's totally the greatest writer who ever *lived*, I mean except for maybe Spinoza, you know? And so that little bitch comes up saying how *he* worships Ellis, and now here he comes, trying to kiss my ass. I don't like that. I don't like that at all. That's what's going on."

"But Will, you're the one who asked him . . ."

"Asked what? Asked who? I mean really, Liz, what are you talking about? Could you please try to make some sense? Oh, honey, I'm just kidding, you know I love you."

That's how Will was acting then. He was always nervously jiggling his leg ("I can't help it, Liz, my leg's plugged straight into my dick"), and he always had a toothache.

He'd whistle through his fingers, he called everybody honey.

Obviously, if you saw him from too far away, or from too close up, it was all what he'd call "too, too"—it was incredibly annoying. From the right distance, though, it was sort of fascinating. And reassuring. He went out every night.

After all those years with Dominique, he felt free.

"Jim, honey, it's like Hemingway said. If you want to eat, you have to use your teeth. Your fucking *teeth*. Grrrr."

And off he went.

"Will, Picasso wasn't the one who said the sky is blue beyond the roofs . . ."

"Oh, honey, who gives a fuck. I mean what's the fucking difference? I mean, ask yourself, here in your own life, whether you think the sky is really beyond the roofs. OK?"

In one way or another, everybody loved him, in the community they treated him like a sort of little kid, he was so naïve. He
wore striped sailor shirts like the ones in *Querelle de Brest*,
twenty years after they'd gone out of style, he'd go up to a couple
of beautiful guys, perfectly turned out, he'd look them up and
down and blow his nose, and he'd tell them, "You have to get
with it. I mean really, you have to at least make an effort. I mean,
it's like Miles Davis said, we're not parrots!"

Nobody knew what to make of him. "What is he taking for
his teeth?"

He was a twerp, but he was an appealing twerp. He knew lots
of people in the community, thanks to Dominique. He was like
a kid you'd watched grow up and come into his own.

"Say, Will, do you like Morrissey?"

"Oh, I love Morrissey. I *adore* him."

Two nights later, for his sake, someone tells the DJ to put on
"Last of the Famous International Playboys" at a party, and Willie, who's smoking in a big group of people, says at the top of his
voice, "I hate that shit. I absolutely fucking hate it. The bitch
sings like she's got a stick up her ass."

He wrote his column in *Blason* in exactly the same style. You
could sum it up as follows: I don't like guys who do things they
think I'll like and think they can think like me. Or else: as long
as I'm the one talking, I decide what's what. If you think you've
understood what I'm saying, I'll say the opposite—get it?

I saw less of him, but I never stopped hearing about him. He
went out with lots and lots of guys.

You'd think you had his number, even I thought so, but no.
That's how he got his kicks. You thought he was on the left, and
he'd say, "No, seriously, man, I'm thinking the future is all about
Giscard. We have to rethink him completely." And your eyes
would widen: Giscard? The center-right egghead who was president when we were kids, and spent our whole childhoods boring

the shit out of us? No, no, he'd go on about how Giscard had actually accomplished much more than Mitterrand, and how we
should bring him back to power, along with Simone Veil and,
most of all, Raymond Barre in the Matignon. And by the way,
Raymond Barre liked the Jews. Whatever. And he could stay
angry at you for two whole days.

People thought he was being ironic, that there had to be
some double meaning. You know what he always said, "Oh, honey,
do you really think meaning comes only in packs of two? . . .
There are, pff, meanings and meanings and meanings . . ." And
he spread his arms wide to encompass the infinite.

Other times it left him deflated, downcast, his eyes looking off into the void, and he'd murmur, "No, there's just one
meaning."

It depended on the time of day.

17

In 1995, after having thrown himself into the debates over the war in the Balkans, which he saw as another Spanish Civil War and which, in the event, turned out to be a sorry mess—witnessed from a safe distance by intellectuals full of phony empathy—Jean-Michel Leibowitz returned "to France," as he put it, meaning his wife and me, and published a noisy little tract about the times we lived in, about the end of authority, the rise of cultural permissiveness, education, politics, political correctness, "the school of resentment," fashion, existence, and time.

The Failure of Intellect, the Intellect of Failure: Moral Bankruptcy and the Ideology of Success.

I told him the title sounded OK. The message was more or less this: Our era is witnessing the end of all intellectual rigor (though it's not as if we're going to outlive our era, is it, and so I don't know why Leibowitz kept repeating the word *era* ad nauseam, as if to convince himself that it existed). In other words, mass democracy, universal education, and access to leisure, to culture, have turned culture into a kind of pseudo-thinking—just a passive, wholesale acceptance of one trend after another.

Leibowitz thought that the victims, the minorities—for example, women, blacks, the poor, homosexuals—had become the pretext for a democratic self-satisfaction. He thought intelligence had gotten mixed up with a cowardly totalitarian political correctness, a habit of saying yes to anyone who'd been oppressed, and to agree with everyone who felt they had been wronged in the bad old days.

For example, we were supposed to like rap, we were supposed to think of it as an art. Leibowitz thought otherwise. Well, to each his own—but Leibowitz thought that saying "to each his own" was a kind of soft terrorism, a deep capitulation of the intellect. He quoted Kant, and, well, in a word, he vented.

Leibowitz never argued that we should outlaw rap. Heaven forbid! He only stigmatized what he called *"la pensée unique"*—groupthink—or lazy, blanket toleration. (Hard to believe there had been a time when he'd say anyone who used the word *laziness* to describe any human behavior belonged to the right.) And of course the expression *"pensée unique"* took off, as we all know. *"Pensée unique"* meant democratic toleration and acceptance of everything under the sun. It dissolved all values, it tore down every hierarchy. Whereas to judge, to rank, was the very meaning of intellect. He thought that democracy had led, as Tocqueville himself predicted, to a failure of intelligence—because, whenever you deal with matters of the intellect, you're dealing with something undemocratic. With inequality, with rank.

The political left, clinging to political correctness once communism died, was partly responsible. I forget exactly why, but it had a lot to do with Mitterrand and his minister of culture, Jack Lang, and the idea of the Fête de la Musique, with everyone strumming his guitar in the street.

He wanted to show that you could understand this democratic failure of intellect by pointing out our weaknesses, our excuses—and so while he was writing he kept trying to show me examples: people we treated as celebrities, as contemporary artists, who were mindless and irresponsible, people whose very mindlessness passed for a deep originality of mind.

So naturally I tried to come up with a counterexample, to show him what was actually new, what was good, about the present day. So.

I talked to him about William, about his slight influence on the community. I explained what was fascinating about him. I said he shouldn't necessarily be judged the way you judge a philosopher, or a real artist, a Victor Hugo, a Baudelaire or whoever. He didn't say anything.

When I asked him about it, he just grunted. I wasn't at all happy to see him use William as an illustration of the "emptiness of contemporary thought" in his book. In fact, it pissed me off.

In the chapter "New Communities and Communions of the Void: Gay Pride, Enforced Pleasure, Scandal as Discourse," William M. represented the "underground," the big "whatever" as the new morality. All you had to do was make yourself heard and represent some "community" in order to become a figurehead, shielded from criticism (at the very least you'd be worth talking about), a star, a celebrity, an avatar. It's no use arguing about such a person—yes, he may be mindless, he may be an idiot, but he *represents* something, he's a representative. And there you have it, there's nothing more to say. It's democratic and anti-intellectual, it tosses aside any canon of judgment, of criticism, of intellect and thought, and it's beyond any notion of values.

To everyone's surprise, this made Willie very proud. I'm not sure how much of it he actually understood, but as I was trying to apologize all he said was "It's cool, it's totally cool." And smiled. "I mean, it gets my name out there. Like a seal of approval, no? Like I was somebody kind of important."

I couldn't quite decide how to interpret the cunning smile he gave me, whether it was supposed to show his higher understanding, his Machiavellianism, and his triumph at having turned the tables, or whether it actually showed that he was tone-deaf and oblivious, indifferent to argument, with the slightly beatific idiocy and triumphant gaze of a fighter who has no idea what's at stake.

18

When Willie got his fifteen minutes of fame, for which he seemed to have been waiting for so long, he played it for all it was worth. Overplayed it. Naturally he ended up on TV.

He went on wearing a skirt, with hairy legs and everything, and a blue wig. He had three piercings and he hadn't shaved. He spent an hour yelling at the makeup women, swearing he'd never go back there again, and covering himself in whole bottles of his own mascara. He called me at the last minute.

"My stomach's all in knots, Liz. I'm totally freaking out. I need you to come here, will you please? My teeth are killing me. Oh God, my motherfucking teeth."

I witnessed the whole thing. How to describe it? He smoked on the set—this at the height of the no-smoking campaign. He yelled, "You peasants! Rembrandt would never have done what he did without tobacco." They posted two fire inspectors backstage—I swear, two of them. Willie was out of control. He flirted shamelessly with the interviewer, he squealed like a little girl, and he bobbed his head up and down, saying, "Totally, totally, I totally agree with this guy Weilobitz you were talking about, yes, totally. I'm totally for abstinence too! And fidelity . . . I'm here to say no to filth. Filth is out. And condoms? Please. You might as well just practice abstinence. I totally agree. No, I mean it! It's totally true. What is the world coming to? Anyway, I say yes. Yes yes yes."

"Um, it's actually Leibowitz. Jean-Michel Leibowitz, who has come out against . . ."

At that moment, I admit, I was afraid he would say something awful, that he'd betray me and say something nasty about Leibo—I mean, that he'd talk about *us*. But no. I don't know why not. It wasn't out of loyalty or friendship, that wasn't his style. If I had to guess, I'd chalk it up to distraction. As usual, his mind was on other things.

"Oh, right. Leibowitz. Leibowitz—he's a Jew, isn't he?"

The interviewer took the bait, naturally.

"Excuse me, are you referring to the gentleman's name?"

"No."

"Well, just what are you trying to say?"

"Oh, I'm just saying, because I'm Jewish, you know? So it's cool. I've got nothing against the Jews. What gets me are all these little faggots you see running around."

"I beg your pardon?"

"There are just so *many* of them. Too many."

"Too many . . . ?"

"But so anyway, I totally agree. I couldn't agree more, I agree one hundred percent!"

The journalists, well, they never said much after that, they just caved. Willie was having fun, freewheeling in front of a full house. He was a natural.

"I mean *faggot* faggots, the ones you see mincing all over the place. I won't name any names, but you know the kind I mean. It's just too much. And look, I'm not saying they should be eliminated, I'm not a Nazi, I'm just saying maybe they ought to stop being faggots! After all, the world is full of women. There's too many, like in China. You can look it up!"

"Too many—"

"Faggots. Too many faggots. I'm totally with M. Leibowitz, and I believe in fidelity."

"And, and so you're saying—"

"Well, just that. That's all I have to say."

He took a drag on his cigarette, legs crossed, and didn't say another word.

All my friends were dying with laughter. Later on that evening was the only time I ever saw a whole nightclub burst into applause.

•

That same week he moved out. And with no one to help him.

I went over and he told me to get lost. He told me, "I love movers. I'm not about to have a bunch of little queens moving my stuff. I *adore* movers."

I looked around at the front hall with its fake marble, its letterboxes, its potted plant surrounded by brown cardboard boxes.

"Well, so how come you didn't call them—the movers, I mean?"

He grunted, bare-chested, as he lifted a couple of boxes. "You can't always have what you want. You just can't."

He'd done it all on his own. He'd found a not-bad apartment, which was a surprise in itself. As far as I know, he never set foot there again after he'd finished moving in.

"It's too grim, Liz. You know what I mean? It's on the fifteenth floor, it's so high up, it's so lonely. Doesn't it just make you want to cry? I can't stand it. I swear, if I go up there I'm going to throw myself off the balcony. I'm dying right now, I'm telling you, dying."

I'd stopped trying to understand. It was just his way, I think, of pushing his solitude aside. He'd been too alone—utterly, utterly alone. He took his boxes, he carried them upstairs, and it was over.

He always slept, he always lived, in other people's houses, the houses of friends or lovers.

I ran into Doum at the paper. He frowned under his thick

eyebrows, he looked down at me a little wearily and, before I could speak, he said, "He's such a pain in my ass. You can't even imagine."

Leibowitz blamed me. And yet he and everybody else thought of Will as a sort of lunatic who'd made a fool of himself.

But as Will said, "You know, Liz, nothing's perfect and nothing's totally lame. Nothing. If something's totally perfect, it's still got something lame about it. No? And something that's totally lame, isn't there something kind of perfect about it too? That's what I like about human beings, you know, and at the same time it's really hard, because, OK, you do something that's completely lame and it's kind of cool too—but that makes it lame, so everything kind of swings back and forth, you know what I mean. Sometimes it makes me want to puke."

For lots of somewhat marginal people, Will had struck a chord. This was obviously unconscious on his part, just as you'd expect. He may have been alone out there, but he was so alone that, in a way, he'd *ceased* to be alone—he represented everyone who felt the same way.

Of course, the more he represented them, the more alone he became.

On and on he swung.

19

For a second Willie just stared into space, then he went on. He told me, pointing down at the letter he'd just opened, "Do you understand, Liz? If I want to keep collecting unemployment, I have to go in for an interview at ANPE, the employment agency—and then what? Do you see the way they're trying to pressure me? I mean, work sucks, why won't anyone just come out and say it?"

"I don't know, Will, I guess everyone thinks it has to be done."

He was in his underpants, eating roasted peanuts. He did that a lot. Sometimes he put on airs: "I'm a dandy, Liz. Once you get that, it's all about elegance, simplicity, sincerity, and purity. You just have to keep that in mind."

He was someone who'd spent so long by himself that he needed always to feel people around him, without ever needing anyone in particular. He made you feel it. He was pretending to smoke his ballpoint pen like a cigarette, rolling his eyes.

"You know, Liz, we have to do something. All this *bullshit* about work, you know what I'm saying? I can't believe people put up with it. Not me. It's simple, I just don't want to. OK, I don't have a theory about it, but fuck it, I don't feel like working like a fucking retard, you know? What I mean is—let's say I don't work, does that mean I contribute less to humanity than some guy with his ass glued to his office chair in front of a screen with numbers on it? I exist, I don't work, that actually makes me interesting to other people. It's kind of glorious. In fact, if you think about it, it's actually kind of selfless. I'm like a guaranteed public spectacle. So why shouldn't I get paid? Really, it's the least they can do. I have the right to tell society to fuck itself. After all, they're the ones who get the free show."

He lay back, staring at the ceiling and scratching his balls. He was restless. He was wearing his angelic face, his daytime face, the one he wore on his good days, when it was just the two of us. I was trying to get some work done.

"Don't bother me, Liz, I know what I'm going to do. I have a plan. Hey, will you cook something? Don't bother me, OK?"

He slammed the door and disappeared into my bedroom.

For a second I actually thought he'd found a vocation. He was capable of anything, he'd come up to you with a great big smile and say, "Tell me, Liz, is it complicated becoming a professor, like your boyfriend Leib? I could get into that. Do you think he could get me a job, like next week? Not *get* me a job but, you know . . ."

You actually had to explain it to him. But whatever, explanations only bored him. He'd burp to himself and go dig up some new passion. He never even listened.

The next day, having made a big production of setting the alarm for six, he shaved and put on a necktie and a suit he'd unearthed God knows where. I couldn't believe my eyes. He slipped a spiral notebook into his inner pocket, gulped down a bowl of cereal, and said, "It's cool, Liz, I'll be back at the end of the day. Gotta run."

I shrugged and put on my blue bathrobe.

He did that for a week. Monday he went off to the employment agency, waited three hours just so he'd be there on time for his appointment with M. Jean-Philippe Bardotti, the adviser assigned to him.

In he marched to the office. Bardotti stood to shake his hand over a big desk piled high with files and a slightly out-of-date computer and various neat stacks of office supplies. He held his long dark tie against his white shirt as he leaned forward, and Will immediately noticed that, seen from above, he had the beginnings of a bald spot. Tsss . . .

"So, M. Miller, what is your occupation?"

He froze. Now Will was kneeling on the carpet, eyes closed.

"Shhh."

"But—"

"I'm saying an old Jewish prayer. I'm praying for you, M. Bardotti."

"For me?"

Jean-Philippe Bardotti, thirty-five years old, was a nice person. He looked left and right, cheeks flushing.

"I'm praying for you, M. Bardotti, so lovely, so lovely and nice, because you're trying to find a job for me, for a poor little piece of shit, for a little turd like me."

At which point Will clutched his skull, pulling out one or two hairs, and started beating his head against the gray carpet. This had pretty much zero effect except for a muffled sound revealing the thinness of the floor, which sounded like cardboard. Bardotti hurried around the table to pull him up, but Will kept going:

"You dirty good-for-nothing piece of pigshit! You lazy, lazy bum! Is this how you thank M. Bardotti, who spends his days working himself to death trying to find you a job? Is it? You little idiot, you exploiter, you bastard . . ."

He shook his head.

"Oh, you are too kind, M. Bardotti. You're too kind for a dirty little whore like me—no, let's not mince words, a little whore. Oh dear, oh dear."

He blew his nose.

Jean-Philippe Bardotti stood there, mouth agape.

"Bardotti . . . That's kind of like Bardot, isn't it? But feminine. Are you related?"

Will smiled broadly, slowly, and he crossed his legs, moving his lips in a strange way.

"Um, M. Miller . . ."

"Call me Willie, Jean-Philippe."

What he was doing with his lips was really weird.

Bardotti was at sea. He couldn't think of anything to say.

"Jean-Philippe, I'm going to be honest with you. As you've seen, I really can be a dirty little slut"—he paused at the word *slut*, then he gathered speed—"the thing is, if you're nice to me, I'll be nice to you. Does that sound good? Wouldn't that suit us both? I want a job. Now."

"A job. Um, yes of course." He shuffled his papers desperately. "That's to say, with your educational background, your uh, degree in sales, well, let's see, it's been a few years now, hasn't it, so we'd have to, I mean, we'd have to adapt . . ."

"I want women's work, Jean-Phi. Do you know what I mean by women's work? I think you do. I think you know exactly what I mean. You're sharp, I can tell."

"Women's work? I . . . I'm not sure what you're getting at."

"Mind if I smoke? No? Well, I mean for example, being a *whore*. Do you have any openings right now for a whore?"

He exhaled into Bardotti's face.

"Um."

"All women are whores, don't you think? Don't you agree with me, Jean-Phi? You don't? You're not wearing a wedding ring, you're not married, you don't have a girlfriend, do you—so you must think so too, no? That all women are whores?"

He burst out laughing.

"No? Aren't I right? How much do you pay for it? You know, with guys it's free, Jean-Phi."

He winked. The next day he was back.

Bardotti hadn't said anything to anyone. He had nightmares about it. He asked himself, Why me? When he saw Will walk back in, I think he would have liked to wall himself up in his own office.

"Jean-Phi, aren't you going to kiss me hello?"

Will was wearing a skirt and tights and makeup, carrying a handbag. He had got up early. He left a big lipstick mark on Bardotti's left cheek.

He took a seat and adjusted his bra strap, wincing.

"Listen, Jean-Phi, I've been thinking it over . . . There's really only one thing I'm cut out for. I want to work in construction. Unskilled labor, if I have to. If not in construction, then in, you know, what's-it-called. You know the thing I mean. With the big tools. The one that goes *brrrr* and makes the holes in the ground, with the cranes and the yellow helmets. I love yellow helmets. Yellow helmets are my favorite."

"Um."

"Do you think you can find me something?"

"Um, well."

Will came around the desk, and Bardotti drew back. Will perched on a corner. "Do you know why I like construction?" He leaned down. "Because in construction, trust me, everything's made of steel. And I mean *everything*."

He looked Bardotti right in the eye: "Do you know what I'm saying?" And he laughed.

The next morning, there he was in a T-shirt and bike shorts.

Bardotti was trembling. He had cleaned up his office. Everything was in place; there was nothing on the gray desk. Bardotti breathed hard, ensconced in his pivoting red-and-black desk chair.

"You let me down, Jean-Phi."

Will took off his leather gloves.

"I told you when I was available."

He counted on his ring-encrusted fingers: "Monday, Tuesday, Wednesday, Thursday, Friday, Saturday, Sunday, what more can I do? First I told you I was ready to whore, then I said it would be OK if you wanted to stick me in construction. Nothing, nothing, nothing."

He paused a moment. Bardotti looked like a large cod caught in the nets of a Japanese trawler. He was hypnotized, he seemed to be swelling by the minute.

Will started to scream, in such a piercing voice that Bardotti actually covered his ears: "I want to work! I want to work! I'm at society's service! I'm flexible." And then, without warning, he took a hammer out of his backpack and whacked his own left elbow, which popped out with a bloodchilling snap.

He collapsed, gurgling, "This is proof of my goodwill, toward ANPE, toward you, Jean-Philippe, my idol. I'm flexible for you, look . . ." His forearm pointing the wrong way, Will fainted.

Bardotti called an ambulance.

He spent three months with his arm in a cast, and was very proud of himself. Everyone came to see him at the hospital. He went on and on about Bardotti: "He's a genius. I love him. If he won't have me, I'll kill myself." He sighed and gazed into my eyes. "This is murder. It's a job in itself, you know."

Two days later, when they let him out of the hospital, after he'd had a thousand red roses sent to Jean-Philippe's office, he rolled up to the employment agency in a wheelchair, carrying a giant padded envelope, wearing a T-shirt that read "I love my social worker." In the hallways he passed out handfuls of bills to the stunned secretaries, to the other workers—then he knocked with great dignity on Bardotti's door. "Please, no," Bardotti whispered, "not him. He's insane." But Will, with his arm in a sling, had already thrown himself at Bardotti's feet. He was kissing them and shaking his empty envelope. "Oh, I beg you, master, I beg you, I don't have any more money, I'm on the street, I'm poor. Oh, how I want to work."

He got back up.

"Or else take me in. I know you have a heart."

Jean-Philippe Bardotti, polishing his glasses, wiping his forehead, stammered, "Why? Why are you doing this to me? I keep to myself, I don't go around hurting people, I don't know anybody."

Will straightened up. "Yes, that's true. Why?" He stroked his upper lip in thought.

Everyone had heard of Jean-Philippe Bardotti in Paris's tight-knit gay community. He had become a sort of cult figure. Willie said, "We need to turn him! He's one of us. He's completely frustrated in that office. We have to save him. Plus, I'm in love with him."

And the next day, Will showed up wearing a T-shirt that had a big pink heart on it, a box of candy in his hand. Thirty friends had come with him. Everyone at the agency was speechless with laughter. Bardotti hid in his office, in tears.

Will knocked. "Darling," he whispered, "it's me." Bardotti's colleagues were gasping for breath.

Will made his way into the office trailed by his entourage, who were singing in unison that song from the eighties, "If I were a man, I'd be romantic . . ."

William, wearing a black suit, proposed and offered Bardotti an official engagement ring.

After a silence, he shrugged. "I could be your housewife. I'll be there waiting for you when you come home at night, with a nice home-cooked meal."

You know, what made Will terrible and invincible back then was, when he said it, he meant it. I'm positive he was in love with Jean-Philippe Bardotti. Really and truly. He was very tender-hearted, in his way.

He came back the next day with a sign around his neck: "Rejected."

He knocked on Bardotti's door. Someone came and told him that Bardotti had left, he'd quit. Everybody thought it was part of the joke, but Will was actually sad. He was brokenhearted for two whole days.

Then he wrote it all up for his column, in *Blason*. It was a hit in certain quarters. Somebody approached him about writing a novel.

"Why did you do it?" I asked.

His toothache was especially bad, he wouldn't stop torturing his gums with toothpicks.

"To make my teeth stop hurting . . ."

He yawned.

"It's nice having obsessions. It gives your life structure, I mean. It's important. If you think for thirty seconds about the human condition, you'll see it's key. You have to be stuck on something that doesn't really seem all that important."

I was drinking tea, leafing through a catalogue for an article.

I stopped what I was doing for thirty seconds, and I looked him in the eyes. "But why do you spend all your energy doing stuff like that?"

He squinted, he stretched (he was worn out), and he clicked his tongue. "Well, you'll see. I'm practicing. I need to focus my obsession."

20

When the presidential campaign of 1995 began to gear up, Leibowitz still counted himself among those intellectuals close to the Socialists. But he couldn't stand the idea of a "pluralist" left. As if *plural* automatically meant "good." For him Jospin would always be the minister of education who'd hesitated in 1989, when he ought to have banned the Islamic veil in the schools. He was promoting a society that had no drive, that was tolerant by default, ossified by the big government of the leftists, gripped by the remnants of Jack Lang's cultural politics, trumpeting postmodernism with all the enthusiasm of an old bourgeois, confusing art with government-funded nonsense, undermining every intellectual authority, every measure of value, in a sordid spirit of live and let live.

Leibowitz's friends ended up saying, logically enough, "It's simple, Jean-Michel. You're not on the left." Leibowitz replied in a furious article, which I got published for his sake in *Libé*: "To be on the 'left' today is to break with the left and its majoritarian spirit." After which he threw his "measured" support behind the right-wing Édouard Balladur, who was prime minister at the time. He even attended one of Balladur's campaign luncheons, where he found himself surrounded by established, rather academic intellectuals.

He wrote various polemics here and there, and he coined the

phrase "majoritarian minorities" which, so he said, was bound to catch on just like his earlier coinage, *"pensée unique."* He used this phrase to describe the ideas of the "left" that, he thought, had quietly come to dominate the media. These ideas had to do with taboos and false generosity, ideas held sacred because they arose from good intentions: antiracism, tolerance, cultural relativism, brotherhood between peoples, pacifism, reverence toward the "economically oppressed." All of which were, first and foremost, theoretical constructions dreamed up by intellectuals.

Somehow the expression "majoritarian minorities" never caught on.

As Alain, his old boss in the Organization, declared, "When you put yourself in opposition to the left, that means you're on the right."

As for the far left, where Leibowitz had once upon a time begun, they had forgotten all about him.

Just when it struck Leibowitz that he really was on the right (in a "critical" way, in an "oppositional" way, not like the others who'd been on the right all along), he was also forced to acknowledge that Balladur had an actual majority, that more or less by default he was in power and that the intellectuals who backed him were also in power, including Leibowitz—and suddenly he went around telling everyone who'd listen that they'd been sheep to support Balladur (though he exempted himself from this judgment). So he swung, through a series of editorials and polemics, to Chirac's side when Chirac had very little support on the right and was way down in the polls.

Chirac beat Balladur in the first round of voting and the socialist Jospin in the second. Suddenly he was president of the Republic.

Leibowitz, a late supporter but a supporter nonetheless, was offered the directorship of Sciences-Po Paris, which he declined, saying calmly that he wasn't for sale. Which wasn't an act. There was nothing venal about him.

Dominique snickered in *Libération* about the president's official "opposition philosopher."

Leibowitz, extremely peeved, answered that nowadays the only way of remaining independent, of fighting against the prevailing *pensée unique*, which never stopped celebrating "minorities," was to be in the majority and to hold office. We must recall Pascal, he concluded. (He didn't deign to elaborate.)

He saw his application to the Académie Française, founded by Richelieu, as an act of defiance toward the false rebellion, as if he were a sort of latter-day Condé. It was also a stand against the linguistic corruption that had overtaken every level of society, to the plastic simulacra of subversion—antiracist, feminist, homosexual—imposed everywhere by the left and the avant-garde and finally by professional activists.

Feeling beleaguered, he gloried in being part of a small minority. The mob struck him as deaf and uncomprehending, while in their eyes he seemed the very embodiment of power, of the majoritarian spirit, incessantly attacking cultural and intellectual minorities. When he watched the news, Dominique liked to say, "In a democracy no one really wants to think that he belongs, intellectually, to the winning side. On the contrary."

From then on he was known as a reactionary thinker, and he never stopped reacting, trying to show—under continual attack, under an avalanche of sarcasm and harsh criticism from his opponents, his former friends—how much this persecution justified him and proved that he'd taken the side of free speech, against *la pensée unique*. It was the only choice for a true marginal intellectual who thinks against his time—who refuses to spit blindly against power and the establishment, the way the rest of them do, the privileged and the limousine liberals, who work the system, all the while calling down the apocalypse, like salon revolutionaries, incapable of taking responsibility for their own actions, shirking the duties implied by their social station. He, quite literally, hated Bourdieu and all that he stood for.

In the pendulum that is politics, contrarian thinkers often find themselves accused, by their foes, of being weather vanes. I can't think where I read that—Leibowitz may even have written it himself.

As for Willie, I remember once he was roaring drunk, shirt off, mid-speech, talking a mile a minute, when he said, "See, Liz, the problem with all your Leibowitz's bullshit about *la pensée unique*, and all that shit about staying in the opposition, is that finally it means you have to be sure you know what the majority is, so you have to know the Zeitgeist, the dominant paradigm—all just so you can think and be against it.

"All he has to say is, Shit, the fags, the minorities have all become mainstream—so, *bam*, that means I'd better go against them, the antiracists, but who's to say that racism or homophobia aren't the mainstream, really? Isn't he stacking the deck?

"Just because you've convinced yourself that you're thinking against the age, against the majority, that doesn't mean you're right—because, well, you're never, ever sure, really, that you understand what your era is, or where it is. That's the thing about the Zeitgeist.

"Shit, what is this era anyway? I'd really like to fucking know. *I* don't know what my era is. Is it gay, or antigay? Beats me. Let me know when you figure it out.

"To think outside *la pensée unique* means nothing. Absolutely nothing.

"As soon as you say it, the other guy says you're the one following the crowd—and maybe he'll be right. And that won't mean you're wrong, either.

"You're all just a dime a dozen.

"As for me, I think you need to be faithful. I'm faithful to the idea of being queer, you know. If it's queer, I'm for it one hundred percent. If the queers announce a Nazi fucking dictatorship to liquidate all the breeders, well, I'm sorry, but I'll stick with the queers. And the thing is, it's got nothing to do with this shit about the majority. That's just bullshit."

He'd had a whole bottle, and he fell asleep almost instantly on the rug.

"Your boyfriend, you know, I think he's basically full of shit."

He chuckled softly.

"If he sees leftists everywhere, that just means he's sick of the left. You only switch sides if you can't get off where you're at. If you were his wife, I'm telling you, he'd start fucking his wife on the side. You know what I'm saying?"

And then he started to snore.

Thanks a million, Will.

21

Will always seemed to be organizing parties for other people to throw.

The big Friday-night party he rechristened Dom/Cop.

Doumé had just been on TV announcing his new safe sex campaign, and he ended his speech by saying, "Be reasonable." That was more than Will could stand.

Shit, you didn't come out to be reasonable.

So he wrote an article, scribbled at the last minute for *Blason*, under the headline "K-POT=KAPO=PAPA." Condom = Kapo=Papa.

Then he went off to a party with this kid named Ali, whom he was seeing a lot of at the time. Will had taken Ali out of prostitution. He said he was training him. Ali was a very beautiful young guy, educated and utterly incoherent.

Back then Will was using protection, definitely. What bugged him was being *told* to use protection. That's at least part of what pushed him over the edge. Dominique had participated, with Stand, in a "prevention meeting" organized by the Ministry of Health in order to assemble, as they said, all the "stakeholders" in the fight against the disease.

"The fucking Ministry of Health," he slurred. "They're Nazis."

He went around all night on Ali's arm, wearing a sign that said "Dom/Cop." Once he'd got wasted, he added with a pink felt-tip pen "(the condomless)" between Dom and Cop. Some people were shocked. That was all he needed.

Willie went on and on about how they were all just sheep, how instead of taking action they just went on their merry way, trusting in the divine providence of the god Prevention and His prophet, Condom.

A few people laughed. Willie knew how to win over a crowd, even if he slurred when he was stoned.

And off he went on an endless riff about condoms.

Ali cheered him on, weeping with laughter.

That's how it all got started. That was all it took. That, and of course all the history there was between them . . .

HATE IS BEAUTIFUL

22

Every Friday night, in the auditorium of the École des Arts Appliqués, Stand sponsored an unusual forum—unusual because it was both a meeting for members and also a kind of open mike where anyone could weigh in. Doumé was the mediator, he was merciless. Everyone hung on his words.

And yet there was a moment when voices were raised to protest the fact that *Blason*'s editorial meetings were taking place at the same time as the board meetings of Stand, as if *Blason* had never been anything but an official organ and newsletter. The question came up during the debate over Will's article "K-POT=KAPO=PAPA," which mentioned Dominique by name.

At first, sure of his power in the movement, Dominique had proposed that they issue a communiqué, on behalf of Stand and *Blason*, censuring William Miller and disavowing him. Then he called for a vote.

It was Doumé who'd established the principle that all participants would vote on every motion in a public forum; and this proved dynamic and useful enough as long as the movement was powerless and unknown, but became suicidal as it grew.

"I move that we censure William Miller's text as contrary, in every detail, to the principles, the ethos, and the bylaws of this association. In purely human terms, what's more, we consider it repulsive. Condoms have saved lives, as everyone here has reason to know. So—any debate?"

At first the debate was timid. Then to Doumé's great surprise—for he certainly didn't see it coming—they turned on him.

The hall was full of curious young gay men—more or less distant from the activism of Stand and Doumé. Even the young guys who shared his views raised objections to the directorship of Doum-Doum, and to the way he had co-opted *Blason*, which until then had been an organ of free expression. The youngest in the hall sometimes even started chanting Miller's name. Doum lost the upper hand. He stood there bewildered.

"I don't understand. It's fine to be angry with me, but to question safe sex? To question condoms? Are you for life, or against it?"

"We're for freedom. We're not dogs on a leash."

I had never seen Doum so lost. At that moment he looked around the stage, to left and right, searching for a familiar face. Rico, Éric, Philippe, Didier. The other founders, and his own generation—all were gone. And he saw that he was almost old. The younger ones didn't understand. It was completely irrational, they were turning against him and tossing aside the one sure thing they had, the very thing that would keep them from dying.

He felt utterly alone.

He tossed his chair aside. He got his feet tangled in the microphone wire. It came unplugged, and you could hear only half his words of farewell: "Well, if that's the way you want it—but I warn you . . ."

He hid his confusion behind a towering rage. I remember how his jaw trembled while he repeated, "I'm going to crush him, just you wait. Wait and see. That's all there is to it, I'm going to crush him, to crush him . . . Shit, shit, shit."

Blason became fully independent and severed its ties to Stand, taking with it the movement's radical fringe.

Naturally, Doum remained the head of Stand, but he had let go the reins of the magazine. In time that would come to seem a mistake—not that he had much choice in the matter.

"Dominique was acting in his own interests. We understand about his relationship with Will, we see the problem, but he let his own feelings intrude in a question that concerns all of us, whatever we may think of Will—free expression, freedom, the very essence of our movement, as Dominique always conceived it. We're not censors."

Olivier more or less became head of *Blason*, soon replaced by Ali.

"Who knows if the guy even knows how to read," Doum muttered. "He's just a fucking puppet."

23

Often in the mornings Doum-Doum would pick me up in his car and take me to an interview. I don't know how to drive. Driving scares me.

He would always offer me a little box of blackcurrant candies and switch on the news. He wore glasses when he drove and, often, for the lumbago in his lower back, he'd wear a big grayish belt that made him look like a paunchy superhero at the wheel. It was rather sweet. It always made me laugh.

"Where to?"

One morning I saw his hand trembling on the gearshift.

"Are you all right?"

He was very pale.

"What's the matter?"

He was afraid.

"I don't know what he wants from me, Liz. I'm scared shitless. I can't handle him."

"What do you mean?"

"He's going to—assassinate me."

My eyes popped out of my head. "What on earth are you talking about?"

He had his hand at his throat, as if to take his own pulse.

"I can feel it."

I thought he was going to faint.

"When we were together, I always used to suggest things—I'd say, 'Let's go to a movie, let's go for a walk, let's go see someone, let's make love.' He spent his time watching me, with those eyes of his, and he'd say: 'Then what will we do?' I was scared shitless. It's ridiculous, I'd hurry to think of something to tell him, to teach him, to offer him. 'Do you want to rent a video?' 'Do you know what kind of flower that is?' 'We're eating in an hour.' And he, he'd say, or else he'd think it, I don't know: 'Is that all you've got?' You took a step, he'd wait for the next step. And I, because I was already sick, I could feel death coming, you know, Liz, I didn't want to hurry. But with him it was like he wanted to explore, to take things to the limit, and then say 'Fuck the limit' and vanish right off the face of the earth."

Sweat was streaming down his face. He was passing out before my eyes.

I needn't have worried, it was a hot flash. He was diagnosed with a heart condition, not a serious one. It was no fun taking him to the hospital. And afterward he never mentioned it again.

24

Here's how I imagine it, here's how he told it.

Willie had met Richard at Dom/Cop, already storied in the annals of Parisian nightlife. A beautiful redhead, a doctor who'd just finished his studies, a bit of a lost soul.

Willie rolled over, grasping the headboard behind him with both hands. He sighed.

"There's something boring about sex."

Richard was putting a knot in the condom. "You said it."

"No, but I mean profoundly boring."

"Yeah . . . wait, what do you mean?"

"Man, sex is over, that's the whole drama of life."

"What do you mean? It's over, sure. Then it starts again."

Richard was lying next to him, and he was hunting underneath the alarm clock for a bag of weed.

"No, I mean in the philosophical sense, you know?"

"You mean 'over' in the sense of having reached its limit?"

"Exactly, Richie. It's just a question of holes and how you fill them, and you always know how it's going to end."

"God, you're depressing me." He laughed. "As if I wasn't already depressed enough."

"And to think we wasted our adolescence on that, you know what I'm saying? We should have made better use of being kids."

"Sure."

"You know, I'd love to fool around like I was still a kid, but all this stuff with holes, in the end, it's not like you've got a million possibilities. When it's over, what next? You know?"

Richard laughed. In one motion he seized a long hair on Willie's chest between his fingernails and pulled it right out.

"Ouch, fuck!"

He giggled.

"What's so funny?"

"I just gave you another hole."

"You're retarded. But sure, I see what you're saying. It's just that, well, shit, everything we do has already been done. Even Dominique's done it."

Richard struck a match to light his joint.

"Pass it here."

They spent the next few minutes happily fooling around with the matches, burning each other, leaving little marks—on an ass, an ear, nipples, testicles.

"Stop, oh fuck, oh fuck."

Then they stopped.

"Shit, it's already over."

"You're not into it, Will."

"Yeah, sure I am. But see, you can't come up with anything. We need something else. Something new. All we're doing is what everybody else does, and I've got a terrible fucking toothache, and all I want is for you to take my mind off it. It fucking kills."

First Richard went and got a toothpick, but it didn't do the trick.

Then he got the apartment door key. Stoned as he was, he tried to straighten out Will's front tooth, to set it back where it belonged, between the others.

"Come on, girls, get in line."

He went to get a knife. Will groaned and his gum oozed blood.

"Hold still, I'm slipping the blade in. Don't move. I'm going to make a lever."

"Ah fu', 'old it 'teady."

"Credit card."

"Ohhh, yeah."

He jammed the card between two incisors, then gently slid the blade in, using it as a lever.

"Ah fu', tha' so goo', ahhhhh fu', tha' so mu' bett—"

They heard a loud crack, and suddenly there was blood everywhere.

Will looked at his mouth in the bathroom mirror, using his arm to wipe away the condensation of his breath.

"You're all right. You're OK. Trust me, I'm a doctor. This is nothing."

"OK."

He fell back defeated on the bed, and turned up the heat.

"So, tell me about yourself."

He sighed.

Richard smoked. "Well, my name is Richard Winter. It's my first year in practice."

"Is it cool?"

"Well, some people like it. I don't have the stamina. All day long the patients come into your office with their diseases. And the thing is, you can see they're dying."

"Dying?"

"Well, sure. What do you think? It's awful, you fix them up, you pretend to take an interest, you sympathize, you treat them and you treat them, and then in the end every last one of the poor fuckers is going to die. Every last one."

"Oh, right."

"It's shit. It's just terrible. I'm telling you, I feel like I can't take it anymore. I'm there, I promise them life. I promise them kids, I promise to cure their stuffy noses. The women blush, they always flirt with you a little bit, and that bugs me. And you tell yourself, fuck, I actually wanted to be a doctor. To be useful, you know. And in the end all you're really useful to is social security. What a bitch."

"Who?"

"Social security."

"Oh, right. Right."

"That's how it is on the other side of the desk, you know? I've got my fucking desk, and they're sick, and I'm life—man, I'm Life. Because I'm the doctor. And I can't take it anymore."

"Hey, come on, you're not about to start crying, are you?"

"I'm sorry. I'm just not cut out for it. I can't. Being alive, taking care of them, it's just not for me. I can't keep doing it. I . . . I don't know, Will, what kind of world is this? What kind of life?"

Will closed his eyes and thought about it.

"It's shit."

"It really is, man, it's shit."

Willie didn't know what else to say.

Richard wiped his eyes. He sat up.

Willie asked him softly, "Are you Jewish?"

"Yeah. Do you have the virus?"

"What makes you ask?"

"I don't know. It's just that . . . sometimes I envy you."

"Why?"

"You can feel death in your guts, you know, it's inside you. You're not behind the fucking desk. I'm sick of caring for people and people, they die, and I don't know what death even is. See, I don't even know. It's just a word. I see people crying sometimes, and shit, for me it's nothing. Nothing at all."

"You've never seen someone die?"

"My grandmother. She was Jewish."

Will rolled his head from left to right on the pillow, clinking his bracelet.

"So what are you saying? You want to feel death. Shit, Bataille said love and death are the same. Dominique made me read the book. It was fucking brilliant."

"Is that really what he said?"

"Uh-huh."

"Will."

"Yes?"

"I want us to do it, you know, *that* way. Without a condom. Like we were making a baby, you know? I want you to do it to me in my gut, like you were making me pregnant."

"You're kidding, right?"

"No. It's true, I mean, that's all there is now. Do you even know what it's like to fuck without a condom? Because the thing is, you know, I've never even done it . . ."

"I know. And all these assholes who lecture us and used to do it without using anything, it's just so unfair."

"Give me a kid, Will. Give it to me deep inside me, give me death, give me the disease. I can take it, you know, and it will be yours, too, a little bit."

"It's true, there's nothing else left to do."

"I love you."

"I love you too."

At least that's how he said it happened.

25

"You still have a toothache."

"Mm." Unshaven in his bathrobe, a beach towel on his face,
in the middle of winter, Will lay on the unmade bed. It was a
Sunday. I offered him what I had, cereal, chocolates, some fruit,
not much. I didn't have it in me to go shopping.

The housekeeper came on Mondays. I looked at the filth in
the cracks between the floorboards and the candy wrappers scattered here and there along with the blanket and a pile of clothes
and one or two boxes.

"You shouldn't eat candy, Will, not with your teeth."

"Mm."

"I don't have the energy to clean this place. Will, do you think
I'm very bourgeois?"

"Mm, you're a fucking aristocrat. The problem with you, Liz,
is that you work all the same. You shouldn't. You do all this stuff,
but you don't do what you need to, to live. It's all for other people. That's bullshit."

I opened the window to smoke while I picked up last night's
glasses.

"Shit, I'm cold. Just leave it closed."

Will was shivering.

I tucked my hair up and sat down next to him. Then I pulled
his mouth open.

"Yuck, you're putrid. It really stinks. Are your insides rotting or what?"

"No' my fault."

For Christ's sake. His mouth was full of blood and a tooth hung sideways. His gum was purple.

"Why won't you go to the dentist?"

"Do' wanna."

I fed him Tylenol, I didn't know what else to do, and lay down in the bed beside him.

"What are you writing there? Is it a book?"

He had a notebook in the bed with him, its pages blackened.

"Uh-uh. It's a battle plan."

"A battle plan."

"To destroy Dominique once and for all."

I glanced at it, I saw wildly elaborate diagrams and—

"Don't touch, don't look. You'll tell him. I know you. I can't trust you. There's nobody I can trust."

I tried to stroke his cheek. "You'll feel better."

He pushed me away.

"Will, why are you like that?"

"I have to go all the way. If I didn't, I wouldn't be me. Now I've got to take it all the way."

"I like that about you, but there's a limit, you could change a little bit, just evolve—"

"No, no, that's bullshit. I'm going to be superfamous, you know? And then I'm going to die. I don't care if I annoy people, I don't care if I piss them off. Anyway, everyone's his own person, and that's all there is to it. Even if they hate me, I'm not going to be less than someone. It's philosophical. I don't give a fuck. I have to be someone who takes things all the way. I need goals."

"What kind of goals?"

"Dominique is plotting against me. But I won't let it happen. The thing is, I can see right through him, he's totally fucking transparent. I know what he's up to, but I'm going to assassinate him."

"Assassinate him?"

"Oh yeah. But not just physically." And he tapped the side of his head, conspiratorially, to signify deep thoughts.

"Don't do anything idiotic, Will, please. Will you promise?"

"No, no, it's deeper, it's more symbolic. Don't you get it, mind over matter. I'm going to use his paranoia. Dominique is paranoid."

"I don't get it, why you hate him this way."

"Because hate's important. It's the most important thing. We live in a society where hate is incredibly underrated. Hate brings you to life. It's everything. Real hate—like Spinoza said, hate is where it's at."

He was windmilling his arms in the air.

"See, I'm going to be famous for that, and if they hate you, even if you die, still it means you're somebody. And that beats love, in a way . . ."

He thought about it for two seconds.

"Because love, you know, love is conquered by death, because of course you don't want what you love to die, but the thing is you do want what you hate to die, and in the end death isn't even enough, because the thing you hate did exist and you can't do anything about that. It's better than death. Love isn't even in the running."

I listened while he talked. You could hear the slow sound of the Sunday traffic out the window, under the gray clouds like wet cardboard, like the fur of a cat.

He kept pushing back one of his teeth with his big thumb, and got himself all worked up laying out his theory:

"Yeah, hate and fidelity are the best things we've got. Look, if you haven't got hatred, you prefer nothing, you choose nothing, you do nothing, you understand everything, and then you're wise, and then you're nothing. Just like Spinoza says.

"You've got to destroy, you've got to blow shit up, you've got to take the shit you hate and fucking banish it from the world. Sure there's something arbitrary about it, no doubt, superarbitrary, but that's because in life you choose, and choosing, you know, is completely arbitrary. As long as you understand that, you're OK. And so for me it's Dominique. I've found mine. I hate the guy. It bugs me that he exists. It bugs the shit out of me. He completely betrayed what was true about the queer movement. He's turned into a kind of total universalist, he talks about victims, and everyone's a victim, and blah blah blah he's going to collaborate with the state, go whining for subsidies, in fucking shackles. He wants to take care of everyone.

"But AIDS was a real opportunity. I mean it was ours, it belonged to us queers and nobody else. He completely diminished the thing. He's been handing it out to everyone. I've seen him at work. I know him, you know."

He spoke with difficulty, spitting, the words piling up.

"We need bad faith, we need to make things up—at the end of the day, really, you're just somebody, you're not the whole world, there's no point pretending. That's morality.

"That's what I want." He made me his witness, pointing to his muscular, sculpted, smooth chest.

"This is what I feel in my innermost being for Dominique. I want to destroy him. I don't just mean ignore him or kill him. No, that would make him a kind of queer martyr, and then everyone would talk about him. No, I want to wipe out even his past and slowly reduce him to nothing. Nothing. As if the guy had never been anything at all. 'What was that guy's name? Who was he, again?' 'Beats me.' That kind of thing."

He nodded in agreement with himself.

"The faggot winds me up and it keeps me going. I'm not talking about run-of-the-mill hate. This is deeper. It's peaceful even, it's cool. It gives a point to life, like a kind of target, almost like something to worship. That's it. I know that I'm alive as long as I push him toward annihilation. It's superimportant. Otherwise . . ."

He was getting angry now, and he sat up in bed.

"Otherwise you're nothing. Shit, Liz. There's nothing. You're something that's going to stop being something. You're going to die. In a way, it's no big deal. But because of that, you know, everything you do, even if you do something really amazing—well, death makes it relative. Totally relative. Because, OK, so you were just this thing, this object. And here are these other people, other things, other objects, lots of them. You see where I'm going with this, don't you? You're thinking, you're listening, aren't you? Because this is some serious shit, you know.

"When you really think about life, I mean when you forget about morality, suffering, all that bullshit, you realize we're all just objects and everyone gets his choice of objects. You choose what you choose. It's as retarded as that, and everybody knows it. And what's more, it's not as if you actually get to choose. Obviously, you've got influences working on you, and plus there's society and everything. You know, Spinoza, all that. And in your life you'll have done this or that, you'll have thought this or that, yeah, but then you die, I mean whether you're the biggest dickhead in the world, or a complete fucking moron or some total fucking Nazi. Him too. It's the same, it's all completely the same, everyone is someone. And that's it, that's the thing. That's all there is, after everybody does what he does, that's all there is to life, it's nothing but that, when you think about it."

He was practically bouncing up and down.

"Really faithful hatred gives you something to hold on to. Without it you're just going to crack. It's impossible to go around thinking that nothing matters. That you can try to do better or worse or nothing at all, it's all exactly the same, and then, poof, you die. You need something to hold on to and focus on. Someone or something, you know, it could even just be an idea—but a person's better—and you try to wish it out of existence, but that's just it—it *exists*, and if you know it's a thing just like you, out there in the world, so what? You still say no to its existence. You focus on wiping it from the world. That's what hate is, it's the coolest thing there is. It's huge.

"And I think AIDS belonged to us queers, it was our trea-sure. It's better to be queer. We're not victims, and death, death is huge, and all this shit about the state and everything is a way of making us believe in the love of women—you know, like Mom, life, she gives you life, she ought to be protected and all that. But no, there's death. Because we're scared. And Dominique, I know he chose that, so I hate him. But you see it's not like I haven't thought it out. It's totally faithful, in a way."

I didn't know what to say.

He finally hopped out of bed, in his underpants, as if his toothache had vanished, and he lugged his laptop into the living room.

"What are you doing, Will?"

"I'm fucking bursting with ideas. Don't bug me. Everything I just told you, I have to write it down."

"You're going to write that?"

"Sure, sure, I have to get famous, I have to hurry, I need a book, right?"

"If you say so."

I was lying down. I was tired out—he'd tired me out. Leibo-witz was at Deauville with his kids. I looked for a book on the nightstand, not his.

"I'm going to write a book, but it has to sell, you'll help me and so will Leibowitz, him too."

"Uh-huh." Then I asked, "Your teeth stopped hurting?"

"Not really, but it's cool. It's going in the right direction. It's going inside."

26

William's book came out thanks to Claude—someone he knew at Fayard.

Megalomaniac Panic Demence H, he called it. Some title.

He was part of the autofiction movement—this thing that started when a caveman got the idea of talking about himself so he could be head caveman, and nobody really listened to what he was saying but still they watched him talk. It continued with Saint Monica's son, Montaigne, and JJR, then when we came along, we moderns, who had nothing left to say about the world, and just put the self onstage. But who *was* this self? That remained to be determined, and then it got to be called "autofiction" when Serge Doubrovsky published *Fils* in 1977. Fifteen years later it had become a style, *the* style: I'm the one telling the story, so I'm in the right. I can lie or I can have nothing to say, but I'm in the right—I have the floor, and that makes a book; William fit right into the tradition. What did I think? I don't know. This was just the way Claude presented it. That's how he sold it. So, well, why not.

So call it autofiction.

Meaning there's no story, just a voice. Someone who speaks, whom you watch speak. So fine. OK. Who's speaking?

For 403 pages (count yourself lucky, I'm giving you the synopsis), there's this confused guy who keeps getting carried away, who says one thing and then the opposite, and who holds forth, for example, on genius, dildos, community, condoms, Leibowitz, meat, and vegetables. For simplicity's sake let's call him William (he just says "I"). In case you haven't got the idea yet, there are no chapters, just "fragments." (Claude's word, meaning there were various sections and Will never made it clear what followed what, because once he wrote one section he couldn't remember the others, and couldn't be bothered to go back.)

As he appears in *Megalomaniac Panic Demence H* (let's call it *MPDH* for short), Willie is a prodigy (an IQ as high as the page count), at age fifteen able to solve the algebraic problems of Grothendieck (he got the name out of the Larousse dictionary). He's a smart kid. A very smart kid indeed. Sometimes he reads Nietzsche.

He has a huge dick, which he doesn't know what to do with (what's the point of a dick? he asks himself), and he jacks off five times a day. Then he does noncommutative topology.

He grows up—that's when things get tricky. Adults think all men are created equal; plus lots of grown-ups know how to solve the algebraic problems of Grothendieck, so that's no longer an advantage, and the ones who can't don't give a fuck, they ask some guy with glasses, who gets paid for that in some university some-place. Fuck! What's the point of being a fucking genius, exclaims "I" (Will). Because Will ("I") is way superior, even if he does say so himself, and that bugs the shit out of the other adults (us, in other words the reader), who humiliate him to get back at him (because he's so smart, they treat him like an idiot, to even things out—and he rereads Nietzsche). They tell him, sure you just uni-fied field theory, and you're a total fucking genius, but you don't know anything about life.

He's totally disgusted, and he says so (I'm synopsizing here—and let me remind readers who are just joining us now that this is *not* a story).

So then a journalist comes to interview him (he's a gorgeous guy, who tells him: You're a fucking genius, man, we all know you can think, now let's see if you know how to fuck).

So then there's a digression on neuroscience: William copies out bits of Changeux, and the Churchlands, word for word, then he ends with a paragraph on transhumanity: the brain is just a bunch of electrical impulses. Thanks to nanotechnologies we're going to transfer it all to processors, wiring it through this and that to a genetically modified dick—we won't have to mess around anymore with bodies. In a few years, for example, we won't have to eat. That will be a thing of the past, and we will be what we are, a brain and a dick. Oh yeah, and there won't be any more women.

Then comes a digression on chimpanzees, politics, power, and homosexuality. We're just a bunch of fucking animals who are going to become machines. At this point the journalist gets tricked in his own apartment, in Paris. William (that is, the one who talks and says "I") has pocketed the journalist's press card (digression on corruption in the press and on the hetero-Stalinism of Pierre Bourdieux). He's planning to steal his identity. Then he realizes, full of rage and hatred, that he's entered into an affair with a (female) bonobo and she's given him AIDS. (For some reason, he didn't modify himself genetically so as to avoid AIDS. But anyway.) The journalist is really hairy, incredibly hairy; then there's a digression on meat: we should all be vegetarians—then a digression within a digression, having to do with Morrissey and *Meat Is Murder* ("Morrissey's a genius, I worship him")—because meat shows a prehuman attachment to the body, to what's between the dick and the brain, it's disgusting, it pumps all the vital energy, and man will become postanimal the day when he is self-sustaining and no longer eats animals at all. Because as long as you keep putting animal inside you, you'll be an animal—like, for instance, women puking out babies.

Then comes the central fragment on hate—but you can read my preceding chapter, which is actually somewhat clearer:

Hate = (love + death) − lies.

The journalist and William are always making love, there's one sex scene after another, in italics. I had to take an aspirin. And then, actually, there's a digression on Spinoza, if I've still got it right, virtual reality and Chaos, because reality is a Chaos that has hooked itself up to the brain, and the dick is God without the Father.

The journalist never wants Will to see him in his underwear—so then Will realizes that he doesn't have a dick, instead he's got a cyborgian nanodildo. Parisian orgies ensue.

The journalist and William get into a big argument because they eat meat (there's a digression on the zoosphere, why Lévi-Strauss got it all wrong about food as a symbolic-political exchange of sex, a passage on the Indians of the Amazon, an extract from the Lonely Planet guide, and why psychoanalysis doesn't exist). It ends with an elegy to purees. Vegetables, the porn star John Holmes and why he faints when he has an erection, a dick that's too long, and vegetarian pâtés with a seaweed base.

It's the kind of book that seems to bear no connection to the world around it, to reality—and yet there it is, existing in the world. It definitely isn't good. It isn't even bad. It's like a bad headache, like something extremely ugly, something badly put together, useless, but undeniably itself. For a day or two it takes up a giant place in your life. There's no point pretending otherwise.

The hero (it isn't a story) watches films on animal behavior, on seagulls, and masturbates continuously. The end. There are even violins.

At one moment, toward the end, the journalist is William's father. There's a cannibalism scene, which leads nowhere. Who will eat the cock? (title of the third-to-last fragment, page 387). A big argument ensues.

Then comes a rather spotty history of the condom, from Louis XIV and lambskin, in parallel with a history of the guillotine since Marie Antoinette. The experience of the Absolute. Condoms as the state up your ass, with the cock as Liberty in a G-string. The character kills himself (is killed) by stuffing his head in a plastic supermarket bag. In fact it's the journalist who assassinates him with a gold-plated condom.

Then comes a digression on "'Dominique Rossi, Grand Protector of Life'—castrating grandmother of queers, defender of condoms (because he can't get it up), and killer. He's going to kill me. Bareback forever.

"I feel his hands on my neck. His latex gloves.

"I'm suffocating, I want to get out. He looks around him. But I'm outside. We'll never make it. We are already out."

It doesn't say "The End," but still, it's over.

It gave me a terrible headache, though I suspect it had no such effect on the few who bought it. I read it all the way through, and it wasn't made for that. Fragmentary writing calls for fragmentary reading.

As for the critics:

Maurice Dantec sent *Les Inrockuptibles* his review from Canada. He quoted a porn star I'd never heard of, Francis Bacon, Deleuze, and Kurzweil. *Technikart* and most of the magazines and "avant-garde" fanzines hailed the emergence of a new voice. It didn't cost them anything. In the chaos of his language, William Miller "produced a spark of pure singularity," something you don't see every day.

The naïve ones took him seriously. I especially remember a short article, a sort of capsule review, that appeared in *Le Monde des Livres*, which read more or less: "This minute's underground literary sensation, the talented young William Miller, presents the fragments of a chaotic coming-of-age, in the confusion of a world marked by sexuality, meat, virtual technology, and romantic hatred. Convincing in its extravagance, despite its obvious lack of technical skill and its lack of substance. Controversial passages will stir debate, if they are read. It shows a liveliness of mind and unnerving flashes of insight—and so allows us to reserve judgment."

The journalist had tried to be fair with this utterly unfair "novel," to tell the truth about a book written in a completely addle-headed trance, without any conscious or unconscious plan, built on a crazy quilt of quotations taken from the Internet or from my own bookshelves, all mixed up because, really, he didn't know the first thing about them—OK, it was chaos. You might say it was chaotic in its chaos. I've given up trying to decide. You can't say it didn't show a sort of desire for freedom. The book was never anything but a symptom . . . William obviously didn't care whether anyone read it, only that they saw he'd written it. The truth had nothing to do with it, that's for sure.

"Not bad, Will," I told him. "You're a writer now."

He snapped his chewing gum. "No, Liz, you don't get it at all. I'm a motherfucking text."

"Ah. Right." And we went back to the television, where they were showing an adaptation of *La Belle Hélène*.

The book didn't do much, in terms of sales, but it made people talk about him, in the community, thanks to the last fragment: "AIDS Saves, Condoms Kill."

I bumped into a friend at the paper who told me, "Wait and see—the thing is a time bomb. It's going to turn into a cult classic. You heard it here first."

It was, perhaps, one of those things known to the few for the essential reason that they are unknown by the many.

We heated up some soup and watched TV.

27

Sidaction 2000 was a kind of made-for-TV media stunt, the point of which was to raise as much money as possible for AIDS research—in the form of individual gifts—an event that over the course of twelve hours wove in skits and variety acts involving artists and celebrities.

Will snickered at the screen. "And here's Dominique playing the good cop in the middle of all that crap. It's like the guy said, everyone's in his place in this best of all possible fucking worlds."

I was waxing my legs, my hair was a mess, I was half watching the TV.

"Hey, Will, want to give me a hand?"

"Shit, yeah, I love waxing."

He kept tickling me. "Cut it out, I'm serious. You're hurting me."

"I know."

"Now pull all at once."

"Come on, honey, I know how to do it."

To distract myself, I looked at the screen. Jean-Luc Delarue in a casual suit, a handful of other presenters, each with a red ribbon on his lapel and a solemn look of pathos, staring each spectator in the eye with the same worried frown—we had to "help." They looked like robots who'd been set to "emote." Whatever, it was the usual.

Will stuck out his tongue at the screen. "What total fucking dickheads. Who the fuck told them to come and bore us with their shit? AIDS belongs to us, it's fucking ours. If you want to fucking talk about it, dipshit, come over here and let me give it to you. Jesus fucking Christ, you talk as if you had it, you asshole. You have to live it."

"Willie—"

"I fucking swear, Liz . . . Look how it all ends up, with this bullshit. Motherfucking prevention, the whole community lining up to kiss their ass and whine for cash. Cash. What happened to the queer utopia? Look at this motherfucker. His face makes me want to puke. Nobody'll ever fuck him. Just look at him. That slut couldn't find an ass to lick, even if he offered to pay. If he wants to get it, he'll have to get a transfusion."

Right in the middle of pulling a strip of hot wax, Will stopped.

"Shit, Will, what are you doing?"

Onscreen, on the white stage dominated by big screens with images of infected Africans, to the strains of "Drive," by the Cars, sitting on the corner of a white cube (white, the color of purity and respect), Dominique was taking the microphone. He wore a red shirt, he had a slight tic in one eye. Will was fascinated by the conjunction of screen and man—and not just any man.

"*Dominique Rossi, president of the association Stand, which is a leading partner in this unprecedented event cosponsored by TF1, France 2, France 3, Canal Plus, and M6. We need everyone's help, everyone's goodwill, to beat this plague. You've been a prevention activist for the last eight years, haven't you . . .*"

In a dry tone of voice, Dominique corrected him. He was sitting between two concerned singers and a beatific-looking rugby player in a striped sweatshirt bearing the word *solidarity*.

"*Well, let's see, 1988 to 2000 makes twelve years, I think. And*

I'm not president of the association, just its spokesman, thank you . . ."

He had all sorts of reasons to feel awkward on the set—his age, his skepticism toward the media, a certain fidelity to his youth. He didn't know where to look—Dominique, who had been such a natural orator—and he fiddled a little bit too much with the microphone. It was like watching a stage actor in a movie. Will was younger, he knew exactly how to look at the camera as if it were you—and you, and you, and you too, asshole. He was used to being on TV.

"Oh Christ, what a loser. Someone should have told him to take out whatever it is he's got stuck up his ass—"

Will choked with laughter.

A strip of hairs dangled from my armpit. "Thanks, Will. You know how to make a girl look pretty." I gritted my teeth and tried to finish the job.

Dominique took a piece of paper out of his pocket and unfolded it with much too much ceremony. As though he were one of Lenin's coconspirators and this were October 1917.

Will kept snickering. "What's he up to?"

"I am not in favor of spectacle. Even now, people are dying. And others are to blame."

He swallowed.

"You'd think he was Giscard stepping down."

Will was convulsed with silent laughter.

". . . we must not close our eyes. In the past we have accused—"

"Ooh, he's getting naughty!"

"Shut up, Will. I'm trying to listen."

"—the state and the pharmaceutical industry. Today, in the very ranks of the victims—"

"Dipshit, you're the victim."

"Shh."

"—there are those who play the role of executioner."

"What?"

"Will, shut up."

". . . *with this communiqué, I take, along with the rest of the leadership of Stand—*"

"The 'leadership.'"

". . . *to publicly denounce the behavior of an individual who, by his actions and his words, commits, today, actual crimes against which . . .*"

Will stared, slack-jawed.

". . . *in the midst of this spectacle of self-satisfaction . . .*" Doum gestured stiffly at the stage that surrounded him.

". . . *we, in our concern for life, for the survival of the victims, wherever they come from, whatever their sexual preferences . . .*"

"What the fuck is he talking about?"

I didn't say anything else.

". . . *their existence, we publicly denounce, for the crime of willfully spreading infection, the writer William Miller . . .*"

Willie sat on the sofa, transfixed, mouth agape.

". . . *advocating unprotected sex, responsible for the infection of at least eleven people, we come before the public with witnesses and with proof. When we're threatened from within, when individuals knowingly kill their fellow men and endanger the lives of the most vulnerable, it is our duty to make them publicly face the consequences of their acts. We will not hesitate in our duty. We are against denunciations, but when we are dealing with traitors, and with murderers, we must respond. There are things we cannot permit. We must defend life—our own.*" He was trembling slightly.

Will was frenetically scratching his head. "The motherfucker. The mother. Fucker."

On the stage they were applauding, without quite knowing whom or what. The polemic was out there. Nothing would ever be the same. The announcer, clearing his throat, murmured his objections to the "rather extreme" tactics of Stand, but he agreed that it was right to speak up against anyone who remorselessly and barbarically tore down those tireless efforts to save lives, because that's what they were doing, they were destroying lives, and it can never be a good thing, and that's what this evening was all about, and please call now, our operators are waiting at . . .

As he was giving out the number, William threw the remote at the screen—so hard I had to go buy a new TV.

"The motherfucker—I'm going to wipe him off the face of the earth."

WHICH SIDE ARE YOU ON?

28

I didn't see much of Will in the early 2000s. He'd stayed in touch with people in the States, ever since Doum first took him. He went back and forth a lot.

His influence over *Blason* was growing and, from a distance, he seemed to have changed quite a bit. I found myself in a low patch, dreading my thirtieth birthday—never a pretty sight in other people.

Since about '96 Will had been a sort of Paris relay for the American underground. He had a good reputation there, better than here: no man is a prophet in his own land. "He's the new Michel Foucault," so they said. In fact, all he wrote were a few obscure pieces, mainly reviews.

Time passed.

Will did regular interviews with porn actors for *Blason*, and the first rumblings started when Will quoted Scott O'Hara. "I'm sick of using condoms," the writer/actor declared. "I'm through with them." This caused some fuss at Stand, and the ranks re-formed around Doumé.

Willie spent his time defending the freedom of the individual, against the moral crusade of those he called "collaborators": the professional institutions devoted to prevention.

It was a dialogue with Aiden Shaw, the porn star, that put the spark to the powder keg. "Today," said Will, "we know that

AIDS is above all the name, you know, of a moral argument that's trying to police our sexuality. All this sex panic, now that AIDS is more or less curable—we can see that it's been co-opted to make the queer community normal, acceptable. That they've assimilated us in order to castrate us. And now when you see a man like Dominique Rossi, a counterrevolutionary of the right, collaborating with the French Ministry of Health, which dates from Vichy, to advocate a universal ban on free sex—well, what are you supposed to think?"

"I can't imagine a 'safe' sex life. I'm the kind of person who takes drugs, who likes to take risks. Unprotected sex is part of that. It's just what I prefer, you know? It's not that I don't like condoms, they're just a piece of rubber, but the difference between fucking with condoms and without them is huge. And it's idiotic to spend years claiming there's no difference."

"That's right," said Will. "They want to ban pleasure, it's completely political. When you hear people talk about murder or crime in connection with sex between consenting adults, one who's HIV positive and one negative, what's happened to freedom? The one who's positive is condemned as a 'gift giver'—and that's moralistic because we're talking about a relationship—for having an exchange of desire, with a 'bug chaser.' It's time that we recognized the political dimensions of skin to skin."

Willie went back to France. He got off the plane a different man. He was a little bit harder, a little bit more distant, he expressed himself better. He wore rings, he had bulging muscles, he'd shaved the top of his head, not the sides, and wore a very light beard. His clothes were by all the latest designers.

He hardly ever called me.

A month after he got back—I was feeling especially down, thanks to Leibo—he told me that he was on his way to pick me up. He wanted to see me. I was amazed to hear he knew how to drive.

As it turned out, he had a driver—Ali, his representative at *Blason*, who'd done a lot of growing up. Years before, William told me that he'd picked Ali up near the campus at Dauphine, where he'd been hustling. Honestly, I have no idea whether that was true. Leibowitz never believed it. Ali always drove without complaining. Will was his friend.

Will rented a limo, like something out of an R&B video. He thought he was a big deal. It took me a while to realize what he stood for, among young people, the ones I didn't know, the ones Doumé could never have introduced me to, the ones who came to Paris from the provinces at sixteen or seventeen, who said, "It was amazing, I kicked the shit out of this backroom guy who told me to put on a condom. Fucking fascists." The anti-AIDS groups were by now completely disconnected from the reality of the gay community, which had become a sprawling hydra.

Will was their idol. He'd sit in the backseat, smoking a spliff. He seemed awfully young, especially next to me. He wore a boa over his T-shirt. There was something about him. He had the aura of a true icon. Really, you had the feeling that you'd seen him in a photo. He was beautiful.

We made the rounds of the Marais bars: Thermik, Mixer, Cox, Duplex, Contrat. At each stop the ranks grew, Will nodding hello. They were just boys, really. And there was an army of them. He impressed the kids. I waited behind him. On the walls, the AIDS prevention posters, put up by Stand in the early nineties, already ten years ago, were framed like souvenirs in a museum. There was no lube, there were no condoms at the register. Will joked that Dominique's old queens would never dare come here, now that the kids were in charge. They don't stay out late, poor things, it's bad for their health. The young guys, sculptural, pierced, as beautiful as high-tech Apollos, all laughed.

"There's a G-string party at l'Arene."

"No," Will decided, enthroned on his bar stool.

"Want to go to Glove? To Transfert?"

"Transfert? Please. Those leather queens still think it's 1970."

Often they'd end up at Le Dépôt. "That's the place," said Will.

He took a crumpled Stand poster out of his pocket: "Sex without a condom—is that your idea of fun?" Under which he wrote, with a felt-tip pen, "YES—what's yours?" and he stuck it up on the wall of the bar.

"OK, let's split."

The jokes all revolved around the organizations, Aquahomo, the MAG, the Gay and Lesbian Center. It was clear that the young guys didn't have much use for collectives. "We're just here to party."

And Will always added, at the end, "It's political."

The others listened, but that was something they never said.

He started to make a speech against the moral order. He was still hopelessly muddled, at least he hadn't lost that.

"All they do is shame and scapegoat us, any which way they can, because that whole fucking generation can't get it up. I already told you that Dominique Rossi—"

I interrupted him. "Will, what do you want from me?" The lights floated around us.

He was chewing on something. "I want to know how Dominique's doing." Then he added, "It's strategic. It's political."

Heading into the gamey stench of the back room, I saw Will starting to pick on a guy in his early or mid thirties for unwrapping a condom. "Why don't you unwrap your little boyfriend here instead . . ."

He took it out of his hand. "Nobody told you? That's how everyone does it now."

The guy shoved him. "Not everyone."

The kids protected Will.

"Fuck, what a fucking buzz-kill."

There were five or six guys circulating through the room, handing out a new kind of lube and free condoms.

"You look like a bunch of fucking nuns."

"So we're nuns. Now fuck off."

They were standing at the entryway, explaining how to register for treatment, giving out contact information for Saint-Louis Hospital, where they'd set up free HIV support groups.

"Ugh, fucking cops. You can smell them from here."

"You're the ones who smell, you smell of death. Get the hell out of here."

The others were still trying to fight back, yelling "Murderers!"

"Old faggots. Get back to your fuck-free zone."

I slipped out, in the confusion. None of this had anything to do with me.

Will came to my house two days later. His teeth were killing him.

He didn't say much. He just sort of moved in.

He spent most of his time on Internet dating sites—I'm networking, he said.

I glanced over his shoulder. Sometimes I felt myself checking up on him like he was my kid.

"What's with you and all these barbacks?"

"Fuck off, Liz. *Bareback*. Not barback. It's serious."

"Well, I beg your pardon. What does it mean?"

"Without a saddle. Riding a horse without a saddle. A fucking stallion. It's when you fuck how you want. *Bareback horse-riding*."

"You mean, without a condom? You give these guys the disease?"

"Yeah. That's it, Liz. That's love. It's like a gift, it's a mystical thing. Spinoza. I fertilize them. Right now I'm putting together these *conversion parties*, across Paris, you know, kind of an underground thing, these orgies where guys who are positive get together with guys who are negative and want to be fertilized. We get them pregnant. Or else it's *Russian roulette*, you know, it's a blast. Maybe it's the *fuck of death*, maybe not."

72482737

"What's with all the English, Will? Is that the new thing?"

"The new thing? It's all new, the community's getting reborn.
There are all these young guys, just like in the States, and I'm
bringing them together. It's my thing, you see what I'm saying,
my role. It's youth. That's where it's at."

"I'm not sure I want you using my computer to send stuff
like"—I leaned over him—"'Juicy hole ISO big squirters, I want
all your cum . . .' Isn't it kind of childish, Will?"

"Fuck off, you just don't understand. I didn't write it for
women."

I lit a cigarette.

"You're *straight*. You're *safe*. And you don't have balls. I mean,
don't take it the wrong way, it's not an insult. It's just a fact."

He was tapping away on the keyboard.

"You don't get it, Liz. You're not part of it. It's pure sex, just a
good free fuck, and when you shoot your wad it's just total fucking pleasure. It's political."

He turned to face me. I was trying to laugh it off—but he
wasn't. He'd left me slightly disgusted. It was one of those moments when you'd rather not be part of either sex.

"Whatever, Will."

"You don't see how boring the world is, you don't see how
everyone goes around pretending. It's like there's a big hypocriti-
cal condom over the entire planet. We're all going to die in the
end—I forget who said that. Now you don't have the right to
smoke, you can't drive fast in your car, you can't say 'dick' to a kid
without getting thrown in jail, and then you've got cops like
Dominique who tell you how to fuck and want queers to collaborate with society, to live, to survive. But fuck, they're like those
assholes from '68 who end up in the Senate, and all the time
they're juggling the wife and the family with the little piece on
the side. Like, come to think of it, someone we know.

"We didn't become queer for that. We became queer because

we say, 'Fuck society,' because we don't want to collaborate, and because we know that if you don't live, you die. You know when you start dying?"

I sighed. I didn't like it when he talked down to me. It was like having some high school dropout lecture you on the truth about Einstein and relativity.

"No, Will," I said, playing along. "When do you start dying?"

"The minute you're fucking born." He was warming to his theme. "Life doesn't exist. We're dying from the beginning! All that exists is pleasure. Neural impulses leading to your dick. It's great to see these young queers who come to see me and tell me, thank you, I'd almost given up. They want sperm, they want *poz cum*. You can't imagine, you've got to risk your life to feel it. Then you really come and it's—"

Somebody rang the doorbell.

Ali had come to get him. I buzzed him up. Will went into the bathroom to get ready.

I gave Ali coffee. He was a mysterious, impenetrable guy.

"Thank you, madame."

I was wearing a shawl, and it made me feel like an old lady, a grandmother with her grandson's friend. *Have a nice time, children, and don't forget to button up.*

"So, you really like Willie, don't you?"

He did. "We're still together. He's a star, madame." He smiled. There was something impertinent about him, though I couldn't say exactly what.

"Right. Do you have the virus?"

He smiled. "Yes, why?"

"Was it Will?"

"Will what?"

"Was it Will who gave it to you?"

"What makes you ask?"

I shook my head. "How old are you, Ali?"

"Twenty-two."

Will came out scented, dressed, resplendent in a black T-shirt. "We're off to an orgy."

I was a distressed mother. All I said was "Don't do anything stupid."

"No, madame."

Will nodded. It was political. "We're not victims. Get off our back."

And he shrugged. "Anyway, when you're old, you take your protease inhibitors and your tritherapy. That's for when you're retired, like Dominique. The days of anti-AIDS establishment blackmail are over, all that shit about high-risk behavior and protection and how you have to take sides. Thank God. It was Manichaean."

He laughed. He put on his gloves.

As Doumé used to say, "The colder the little bastard gets, the more beautiful he is."

"Oh, hey, Liz, I forgot to thank you. I borrowed some cash." He laid a video on the glass coffee table.

"That's the film with Tony Valenzuela that I helped produce, *Bareback Rider*. I've got a cameo. Tell me what you think. And feel free to show Dominique. He used to like videos, back in the day. Ciao, and have a good 'fuck'"—he made quotation marks with his fingers—"with Mister Decadence. Don't forget to use, you know what I mean. Think of his wife. You can't be too safe."

"Fuck off."

Ali shook my hand with an air of ironic respect. I could see the way my apartment, my manners—well, to him I was just a white bourgeoise.

I went for a walk in the cold, I was alone, I went without hat or gloves. The icy air almost burned, and I stayed out for a long time, numb, drunk, as if it would have been worse to go inside and warm myself by a fire, by a hearth, by a radiator, indoors.

I remembered something Will had said, two or three days earlier, beside a crackling log, while he skimmed an article written by Doumé for *Libération*, where Dominique expressed the wish that young people would save themselves from the fate of the older generation, and do it by choice. Will tossed the newspaper into the fire: "Dominique, that old whore. He wants the next generation to profit from his experience, not to make the same mistakes. You see, that's the thing, he's just like a fucking father, someone who doesn't understand what it means that *you were born*, someone who wants to take revenge on you because you were born after he was and you're going to outlive him, and his stupid fucking life won't have meant anything. You were born, for fuck's sake.

"He tells you not to do the same stupid things he did because he's trying to convince himself that there was a point to his having done them, for everybody else, for posterity. Posterity doesn't exist. We'll do the same stupid things he did, and all the same stupid shit he suffered through, we'll suffer through too. It won't have served any purpose, except for him—and he'll be dead.

"Nothing you do serves as a lesson for other people. What you do only matters to you. In the end, everything that you accumulated disappears, poof, because you die. That's what they're all trying to hide, and that's why they all lie. They're afraid. They're protecting themselves.

"There's no morality outside the self. You're not responsible for other people. You can't teach them anything and they don't teach you anything, either. And actually when you come, it's you. It's just you. There's no way around it. You know you're doing it for yourself. That's the pleasure of it, that it's all for you. The feeling can't be communicated to another person. Sometimes it may be *coordinated* with another person, but that's neither here nor there. You spurt out some cum, but it's basically a matter of chance. To each his own cum, you get what you can, you make the most of it, you die, and it's over."

He pressed the ice pack against his swollen jaw.

"Otherwise, we wouldn't each be our own person. It's cool this way. It's cool. There's no condom against death. I mean, you might as well live in a plastic bag and pretend you won't end up in a coffin."

29

Will spent the year 2000 absorbed by the Web. It was all he talked about.

"It's kind of like Spinoza, but concrete, everybody linked together."

"OK, Will."

One of his first and last Web stunts was to put up, from my computer, thirteen photos he had of Doum-Doum, which he'd digitized with my scanner. "Excuse me, Liz," he'd asked innocently, "do you know how to make a website?"

I called Antoine, the head of our multimedia department. Before that he'd been webmaster for a music label. I'd been flirting with him, kind of, and he was wrapped around my finger. Will simpered and hit on him mercilessly. Poor blushing Antoine kept trying to explain, "On Dreamweaver, to start with, if you're a beginner, you can also—"

"But if I push that one, there, what does it do?"

"No, hold on. I explained, you don't do that yet."

"Oh, but I thought you told me you push that one, so I pushed it."

"Just wait a second."

"OK, OK. I'm waiting . . . Wow, it's all so interesting. But so, if I want to put that there, I can—"

"Wait!"

So anyway, Will had his website. I don't even think it was premeditated, he just filled up a whole Dominique Rossi page with "some reflections on the AIDS saint."

The headline, in red on black, was something Dominique liked to tell interviewers: "No one can say that Dominique Rossi never came without a condom."

Will's commentary: "double negative? triple?? any-1 here know grammar???"

And he posted thirteen photos, each with a very short caption, no more than a line.

It was full of sadness and nostalgia—at least that's how it seemed to me.

For Dominique, I imagine it was an act of insane violence.

For the others, the militants, the youth, the community, it was truly, incontestably funny.

@1. The first thing you saw was a Polaroid in the center of which a man's hand, recognizably Dominique's because of the large ring he wore back then, stamped with an S, stretched out a penis, his own—soft, limp—from a mass of dense pubic hair, black and strikingly thick. Next to it he held a ruler. Will wrote, "He was supposed to be so good in bed, but with 11 cms—at a 'stretch'—it must have been a matter of technique. Dig the afro. Wasn't he the one who wrote a hairy dick was halfway to a pussy?"

@2. Second Polaroid. In a dimly lit bathroom, surrounded by laundry and toiletries, Dominique crouches on the edge of the tub, jaw out, scratching his armpit, hanging with one hand from the showerhead, imitating a monkey. He's naked and looks like an idiot. You can tell he lets himself look that way because, in the moment when the viewer took the photo, the viewer loved him and they were by themselves. Will wrote, "I always knew we got AIDS because somebody horny fucked a chimp."

@3. Better quality. Dominique sits naked on the toilet (in what friends would recognize as the Saint-Paul apartment), making an ecstatic face. In one hand he holds Leibowitz's book *Fidelity for Life*—in the other, a few torn-out pages. His ass is slightly raised, he's in the midst of wiping. Will wrote, "Way to treat a friend! That old arriviste Leibowitz has been waiting for his buddies to get him into the cabinet—guess the toilet will have to do."

@4. Dominique, out of focus, is on all fours on the rug, a dog collar around his neck. His tongue is hanging out. I looked hard at this image. What troubled me most was that I was sure, contrary to what anyone who saw it might think, that there was nothing sexual going on. Dominique used to fool around, barking like a dog, and Willie must have thought it was funny, so he took the picture. Will wrote, "Dominique wrote: 'The time is over when to be homosexual was a humiliation.' You've rolled over, Dominique. Now let's see you beg."

@5. Fifth photo: very sharp focus. Doum, naked, holds up a large photograph of a dozen men, Stand's Vigilance Committee, like a placard. Someone has written in Magic Marker on their faces "tiny dick," "rice queen," "sucks piss," and other more or less legible insults. Doum wears a bowler hat, and something about the way he holds the photo makes him look like a salesclerk selling lingerie. Will wrote, "Everybody's friend, especially at an orgy."

@6. Doumé, once again stark naked, wears a black kerchief on his head and a large hoop earring. He looks like the Moor on the Corsican flag. A young Willie is on his knees, wearing a liberty cap, he seems to be made up like Marianne in a tricolor skirt, blowing Dominique. The picture was taken with a self-timer. Will's comment: "This was before Dominique got in bed with the government."

@7. Dominique on a bed. He is making love, in the missionary position, to what is clearly a blond woman. Will adds, "A good representative of the queer cause—especially with the ladies."

@8. Dominique and Will are squinting, apparently into the sun, their faces badly framed. They must have taken the photo themselves, at arm's length. You can make out the Giudecca, in Venice, behind them. They're smiling. Will looks so young. Doumé is holding him tight, and there isn't a single wrinkle on his forehead. You can even see his freckles. It looks like they were having beautiful weather. Will didn't write anything under this one.

@9. Dominique is taking a piss in the forest. He's wearing a big fur coat. Everything around him is covered in frost. The photo is in black and white. He looks beautiful. His profile stands out against the whitened trees and his breath makes a little steam cloud before his eyes. Will's note: "You'd think he was looking at his soul."

@10. Dominique, tired, face drawn, wearing a T-shirt, pants around his ankles, slouched on my cherry red sofa, penis out, looks at Will behind the camera and gives him the thumbs-up, as if to say, "Not bad." On the TV screen you can see a porn shot, hard-core by the look of it. The actor is awfully young. I must not have been there. I always left them with the keys. Doum's penis is flaccid. Will remarked, "Too bad you can't do it with your thumb! Dominique Rossi hasn't had a hard-on in five years. Surprise, surprise."

@11. Close-up, overexposed, of Dominique's stomach, his abdominals flabby with three rolls of fat. Will: "Have another beer!"

@12. Dominique, without an erection, is having his dick sucked by a young black man who is simultaneously trying to jack him off. He looks exhausted, his face pouchy. Naturally his belly is hanging slack. He seems to have no interest in what's going on. He even seems slightly disgusted, the room is gloomy and dim. Under the young man's fingers Dominique's sex doesn't seem to be doing much, it's soft, and he isn't wearing a condom, and Will concludes, "We can't say it often enough: Dominique Rossi has never come without a condom."

@13. Last photo: An old Polaroid of Dominique Rossi all dressed up, as if for somebody's birthday. He's holding an inflated condom like a balloon, glowering as he pushes a large sewing needle into the latex. Behind him, a sheet and a bed. New York, maybe. Will ends: "Dominique Rossi tests a condom. So, does it work?"

I couldn't imagine how he must have felt when someone told him to take a look at what was on the Web. Everyone in Paris had seen it. Everyone was joking about it. At Stand they weren't too pleased.

Willie said, "It's like Gide said, intimacy is what we call the tricks we can only play on people behind their backs. It's the least a queer can do."

"Oh, Will, what are you talking about?" I asked him sadly. But he'd already moved on.

I said, "Do you realize, Will, that since it's on the Web everybody's going to see it?"

"Oh, Liz, the Internet is so over. It's done. You have to keep up. It's ancient history."

And then, "There's no joy to the past, it's always sad, even when it used to be joyful. It only proves that the past is shit. The best you can do is forget."

30

With the last little group of his friends, Dominique launched a coup within Stand. He got some of his inner circle appointed to the board, and he called for emergency measures to exclude supporters of the barebacking apostle Miller, guilty of crimes against humanity.

It was this last expression that stuck in everybody's craw.

Even if its influence had diminished in the last few years, Stand was by then a sort of institution, occupying a comfortable building in Aubervilliers purchased three years earlier with an inheritance from Philippe, whose collection of surrealist works, erotic photographs, and Breton memorabilia had been sold at auction.

One Thursday night in 2001 there was practically a fistfight. Ali led the attack against the old guard. His three main complaints: the authoritarian attempt to take back a movement that Dominique no longer controlled; the libelous and very serious misuse of the expression "crimes against humanity" in connection with William Miller; Dominique's total confusion, very counterproductive to the movement, between personal feelings and the politics of the association.

Furious, Dominique lost control. He got up and ranted against the Internet, against homophobia, the plague of the Web.

Inevitably, people laughed.

"The whole life of the organization is online . . . Are you saying we should accuse ourselves? Are you saying the Internet is fascistic and homophobic?"

"Of course I'm not saying it's all homophobic, only that it tends that way."

By now the kids were cracking up. "Come on, Doumé, maybe it's time to upgrade from Minitel?"

Dominique raged and shouted, and the vein throbbed in his neck like a pink rope all the way from his ear to his shoulder: "Have you lost your moral sense? Everything's going to hell, don't you see that this guy is destroying everything I—we—have worked to—"

"Woof, woof." They were barking like dogs. Some in the back were making chimpanzee noises.

They were having a field day.

"Hush, Dominique. I'm not sure you're in the best position to give us a sermon on morality." This was the "rice queen," a.k.a. Thierry. The last of the "old guard," that is, the gang from the eighties, didn't think much of Dominique's relations with Miller. They weren't about to forget that photo of Dominique and the placard.

Dominique, beside himself, his fingers fiddling with a little piece of paper, finally came out with several accusations against Ali that until now he'd kept to himself.

"Your parents . . . Hossan Hassam was close to the Muslim Brotherhood, wasn't he? Didn't he write—"

Ali shrugged. People hissed. "You know I broke with my parents. Do I accuse you of supporting the separatists in Corsica?"

"And where do you stand in connection to the Republic? You made the association sign the Islamist Banlieue-Palestine manifesto, and the veil—"

"You're being hysterical."

They were booing Dominique.

Ali went on. "There was nothing 'Islamist' about the manifesto. Why don't you go join your friend Leibowitz. You and he
clearly share the same imperialist, ultra-Zionist worldview—or am
I wrong?"

Everyone knew Doum supported the Palestinians.

"Don't talk that way about Jean-Michel Leibowitz, please
don't. His parents—"

Now Ali was standing. "I'll tell you what you can't stand,
Dominique. You can't stand it that I'm going out with Willie
Miller, your old lover, that's your problem, you can't stand to see
a Muslim going out with a Jew, and you call William a fascist, and
you call me a fascist, meanwhile you're ideologically at sea, you're
completely passé, and you—"

"I didn't call—"

"Let me finish. You're the fascist here, you and your friend."

"How dare you—"

"Let me finish. What's your position on the conflict in the
Middle East? Your categories are obsolete. Stand has joined the
struggle against the occupation because we believe in solidarity.
A Palestinian today is like a queer under a homophobic regime.
We're in the same struggle. Times have changed, like it or not."

Doum counted his last supporters. The nearly luxurious
building, the fourth floor with its meeting room, the drinks and
snacks on the white tablecloth . . . Two guards had stood downstairs ever since a vandalism attempt the year before. They were
supposed to be a community, and yet he had just ten supporters
left, and those were wavering—as he noted.

The next day the founder of Stand announced his depar-
ture from the association, citing irreconcilable differences in
ideology.

"Stand willfully closed its eyes to criminal practices that ruin
the credibility of the community and destroy it. That was the beginning of the end, and the signature on its death notice. Today

we see the result. Stand has turned away from the mission of prevention, support, and public activism, engaging instead in demagoguery and ideological grandstanding. I wish the association luck."

Dominique went back to his job at the paper—but having lost contact with nightlife, he couldn't really cover the beat. "I'm tired, Liz, I don't feel like going out every night. The music gets on my nerves, it's turned into crap. They're all into this techno stuff now, it hurts my ears. It's completely superficial and irresponsible. When they fuck, all they think about is death, and it's so childish. I can't watch it anymore. Paris is rotten through."

For a brief time he moved in with me, completely at loose ends. "The page has turned." He kept remembering things from his past. I made a habit of putting them on tape.

The friends he loved were dead. The others he'd lost when he distanced himself from the community. It was like the silence after a concert that had gone on for years.

He drank his bourbon. He missed intellectual discussions. He couldn't really have them with me, not really. In many ways he tried, we tried. But it didn't work, of course. That's not who I was.

"I'd like to see Leibowitz again." But Leibowitz would never have agreed to see him, not now.

31

Everything came together and made sense in Leibowitz's head. He thought in terms of *positions*.

September 11, the Islamist attack on the world-dominating USA, symbol of the West; a new suspicion of traditional European intellectual values; the antiglobalization movement, the left reconstituted with a rhetoric of oppressors and oppressed and of wealth redistribution; the conflict between the Jewish state and Palestine—and the attack on his person launched by Ali, the new spokesman for Stand, the derelict queer organization, which had accused him of being "Zionist." The way Leib saw it, the victims had become the executioners.

If they accused him, of all people, of being a Zionist, and if a homosexual of the pro-Palestinian left called him a Nazi, by implication, because he was a Jew—then this must indeed make him Zionist, and a proud one. He had no choice but to defend Israel and the United States.

Leibowitz wrote one of his biweekly columns for *Le Figaro* with the headline "Anti-Semitism, the Left's New Cause."

Far from the declarations of Likud's loose cannon, Ariel Sharon, Leibowitz maintained the same position he had held since the Yom Kippur War. He defended Israel's right to exist while recognizing the Palestinian right to representation and the need for a just peace.

But it seemed to him that an anti-Semitic, anti-American strain of radical Islam had gained a foothold in the French left and especially in the movements of historical minorities, who were always prone to delusory identification with the oppressed. He detected a secret link between the irresponsibility of militant, radicalized "Millerian" homosexuals and modern anti-Semitism. He reread Genet, he delved into the roots of the evil, and a friend of his on the right said, "He's interested in the world as it appears in his head, but when it comes to the facts, the outside world—he's out of touch. It's too bad. That's the danger for intelligent people who spend too much time thinking."

Leibowitz had lost all his hair.

TRUE LOVE

32

Toward the end of 2001, at the height of the phenomenon, everyone—everyone in the media, that is—was waiting breathlessly for William Miller's new book of "autofiction." The publisher, Grasset, promoted the book according to a time-tested strategy, by describing it as "the opposite, but the same."

Here I briefly enter the scene.

Miller was now much better known and more important than Dominique, whose existence in people's minds was mainly determined by what Miller said about him. Ever since William and Ali had more or less publicly broken up, and Will had left to found Le Mouvement PD Dur—the Hardcore Queer Movement—people were expecting an incendiary book from Will about Ali, Arabs, the left, globalism—or else something about the Socialists, Dominique, prevention, and the state. Or if neither of the above, at least a big brutal book about the right, homophobia, Leibowitz . . .

But no. He'd written a book about me.

My Friends Are My Enemies. Elizabeth L., a manic-depressive journalist working for a depressing paper.

The publisher described it as "alterfiction."

The book was one long hatchet job about me, my closeted bourgeois side, my droopy breasts, my vagina, women, cows—and my affair with a tall, bald intellectual. Everyone recognized him.

According to public opinion, the book was shit, basically a first draft, unreadable, utterly uninteresting. Obviously—I *am* uninteresting.

Frankly, I've never really understood why he did that. For him, falling out was a form of love.

Later, when I asked him how he could have acted like such a prick, Will answered, clutching his jaw in bewilderment, "It was meant as a gift, Liz. From the heart."

So be it. I spent a year on disability, dead, tranquilized. Leibowitz stopped calling. He was busy trying to patch things up with Sara and defend his honor, for the children's sake.

I'm incapable, even now, of reading the whole book. It's the kind of nonsensical rant Will used to launch into when I met him, against women (cows), against journalists, the bourgeoisie, depression, big apartments (which he certainly put to use). At the end I killed myself.

The reason I forgave him, after six months, was simply that he'd "forgotten" all about it.

Will seemed happy with his coup. He was a little less in the public eye, his breakup with Ali had let him get in touch with his Jewish roots and read the Torah. "I always loved Spinoza."

I got over it, bit by bit.

A few sentences have stuck with me.

"She had the sourness of women who will never have little boys, who will never appropriate male sperm and tell themselves they're creating life—women who are the creators of death. Women are dead, women like Elizabeth L. They take no pleasure in sex, for they have no sperm. These are the mothers of bitterness. They are pathetic."

Will was incapable of being malicious, I believe this sincerely. He didn't really believe in the existence of other people. He thought of his life as an experiment, and he expected no truth, no judgment from other people.

He smiled at me, one last time. "Why did I do it? Same reason as everything else. No reason, just to see what would happen. *No offense.* Shall we?"

I don't hold it against him, I never did. I had only myself to
blame.

33

The problem, when you have a problem with someone, is that there are others all around you. Yes, there are times when this is a good thing—but not really when the other people are Dominique.

I felt as if I were caught in a spider's web.

Each of them had tangled his feet in the other's threads, then each accused the other of having set a trap, the threads got tangled, and the more time passed, the more they resembled the sort of old knotted bits of string you can't separate without cutting.

What got me most of all was the article Dominique wrote.

When I was at my lowest, after William's book came out, Dominique took it on himself to attack it in the paper.

"For the Honor of Elizabeth Levallois."

Calling William a Nazi, accusing him of helping to establish intellectual concentration camps, he spewed a litany of insults, meanwhile recalling that I had helped him, that I had got him started, that I'd given him shelter, fed him—in a word, it turned out that I was, naturally, the one to blame.

After it came out, I aged overnight. I cut my hair and went into analysis.

Obviously the article in my defense was, in fact, an attack on William. Dominique found himself extremely isolated at that point, and William had truly reduced him almost to nothing. He was thin, and his head seemed to be almost nothing but skull. He was living "with friends," an apartment he more or less squatted in near the Parc de Sceaux. He smoked a great deal. He continued to fill a more or less honorary position at the paper.

William had become a true obsession for him. He came up in every conversation. He said he was doing it for the community, he was taking a stand against criminal behavior, and this of course wasn't untrue.

But. I loathed the article. He used me to pour his bile on the other. Under the pretext of defending my honor, he laid out everything I'd done for Willie—and most of the people around me, colleagues or parents, shrugged: You know, they said, it's a little bit your fault, if this guy actually exists. You made your own bed.

I went to see Dominique at Sceaux. It was good for me to go out, to take the train. I rang the bell, in my dark glasses—and someone opened the door for him. Someone I didn't know, a rather elegant woman, some kind of academic, perhaps a friend from his university days. She asked me to come in. It was one of those beautiful houses with window boxes, like a miniature bourgeois château. She was well-bred. The sky was mauve, very clear. I stopped on the doorstep to admire the sedan parked on the gravel.

Dominique came down in shorts, he looked truly happy to see me and happy to have a visitor.

I let him have it, though I don't remember quite what I said, and I slapped him across the face. The way you do when you want to be angry. When you're really angry you make less noise, you don't have to convince yourself.

I of course reproached Doum for everything I couldn't say to Will. Doum was a normal human being. Dominique replied that I protected Will too much like a son, but it seemed to me he said that partly as someone who could never have a son. Neither could I, he might say, which would be cruel—but I'm the one telling this story, so I get to have the last word.

It was unfair.

Everything that was bothering me I threw in Doum's face.

In retrospect, I think it must have hurt him, because he thought I was coming to thank him.

"All right! I'll never try to do anything for you again. Get out of here, go back to Leibo, ruin your life with that asshole like a substitute husband and that other son of a bitch like a substitute son. Go on—"

"Yes, Dominique, that's right," I shouted back at him, "and with you, you lousy bastard, for a substitute friend!"

Suddenly he was calm. "Ah, no," he answered very coldly, "don't think of me that way anymore—you woman." And that was very insulting.

He closed the door.

In the upstairs window I saw the woman, slender and beautiful, who watched me through the muslin curtain, like a ghostly head in the corner of the windowpane above the three silent red window boxes.

And I walked away in tears.

As a woman, I've had so many male friends who loved only men that I've grown accustomed to feeling useless. It was true I had no husband, no children.

And for years I saw no more of my good old friend Doumé.

34

William lived here and there. He compromised himself by writing any old thing for any magazine that asked. He demanded a fee for every scrap he wrote. He needed the money for drugs.

He developed a serious stutter in 2002.

He grew a little beard. His new clothes reeked of money. He would wear lots of rings. He may not have known how to keep anybody's love, but these things are relative. As famous as he had become, he could afford to get into trouble. I worried about him—when the platform of his celebrity gave way, he'd be at the mercy of people who couldn't stand him anymore, and they'd tear him to pieces.

"I'm huge now"—he yawned—"I don't even know if it's worth writing a masterpiece. What's the point?"

Stand had more or less imploded after the presidential elections of 2002: faced with Le Pen, did they have to endorse Chirac? Willie said none of that interested him anymore. He walked around with his Torah.

"Ever since they called me a Nazi, I've been feeling awfully Jewish."

He snickered. It was the moment of his greatest importance—mediawise. But as often happens, he was already on the way down, if you took a closer look.

William was the head of a penniless organization—all its

funds went straight up his nose. The MPDD was in reality nothing but the Millerite Party to Destroy Dominique.

William wanted to bring together all Dominique's enemies—*my* friends!

The more he lost his grip, the more he talked about him, if it makes sense to talk about him ever having had a grip on anything.

The youngest had had enough—they'd never even heard of this "Dominique."

The youngest sided with Ali, who took various far-fetched positions, but at least they were actual positions.

Sure, William still had his inner circle. Through connections he'd come to edit a sort of imprint at a small publishing house, where he published whatever he got hold of. He always started off on good terms with his authors, then somehow things would go south.

He took it as a joke. "Me, who couldn't even spell my name, and always got such bad grades in French. Shit, what do I know about literature?" He stopped, as if he had marbles in his mouth. "But I do have power, you know, real power."

In the press release that announced the official birth of the Millerite Party to Destroy Dominique I found that I was listed as vice president. The little bastard claimed he had Leibowitz as his treasurer. Leibowitz denied it.

The whole thing was a flop.

Nobody cared anymore about Dominique Rossi, and people were starting to care less about William Miller too.

The wave passed. There weren't all that many ways of staying afloat.

35

"Here I am with William Miller. It's good to have you on the show."

"Yeah, you just said that."

"Yes, of course. But now we're on the air."

"Oh, yeah. Cool."

"So, William, there's no book, but you've come to talk to us about a new imprint that you're launching. A line of erotic literature, am I right?"

"No way, you've got it all wrong."

"That's not it?"

"No, but I mean, you're in radio, right? Like queer radio?"

"This is Radio Attitudes—"

"Right, whatever, Gay Attitudes, whatever, my point is, you're like kind of alternative?"

"Yes."

"Well, right, so you want to do some kind of promotion, right, and I'm not interested. The stuff you're talking about, the books, they're strictly for whacking off, but you know, you have to pay the bills, am I wrong?"

"Well, so you're saying you consider this more of a mass-market thing, rather than, um, erotica?"

"Sure, they're stroke books, but anyhow, it's completely over. On the Web you can see any video you want, I mean what's the point of books, with words? All that's over, all of it—I mean the Web too. There's even more words on the Web, if you think about it."

"Ah. Right. But so . . . how come you're publishing these books?"

"Well, you've got to feed the machine. Plus fuck it, just to see what happens. There's no real reason."

"OK. Well. We can come back to that later."

"Sure, whatever."

"Are you working on any other projects?"

"Not really. I mean, 'projects'? Projects are for idiots, people who think they're going to die."

"And you don't think you're going to die?"

"Me? I'm already dead. They've killed me."

"They've killed you."

"Shit, yeah. When you get AIDS, you know, there's always someone behind the gun."

"You almost sound like someone from Stand."

"Huh, yeah, I'm glad you said that, because you know, people forget, but I really dug Stand and what they did."

"You're, you're kidding, right?"

"Do I look like I'm kidding? Dipshit. Cynical little fuck. I'm telling you I was there when the thing was fucking founded. Stand fucking ruled. It was one of the best things that ever happened to the queer nation. For real."

"OK. You were saying that you felt as if they'd killed you."

"Well, no one's going to be surprised to hear me say that I'm currently the target of an organized assassination attempt, personally planned by Dominique Rossi, and I've got ways to prove it."

"That's a pretty serious accusation."

"Right, but that's not even what I'm saying here. The problem isn't that this guy wants me dead, it's that he's already killed me, you know."

"I'm not sure I'm following you."

"Dickwad. You think I got it jacking off?"

"You mean, um, the virus?"

"What else."

Silence.

"You're trying to say this is the guy you got it from?"

"Sure. Obviously. You didn't know? OK. Well, that's what happened, Dominique Rossi fucking spiked me with his love juice. Mind if I smoke? Thanks."

"Is this . . . something you can prove? Can you remind our listeners who Dominique Rossi is—I mean was?"

"Right, right. The founder of Stand, which the younger generation wouldn't have heard of, an organization for protection and prevention. He's the guy who, along with the Ministry of Health, launched all the condom programs. Maybe that rings a bell. Young people really don't have much culture nowadays."

"And?"

"OK, look, Dominique Rossi is kind of like a dad to all of us, you know what I mean? And, well, we were together for five years, as a couple, an old-fashioned couple. He was HIV positive and at first he didn't tell me. We didn't use condoms. Is this clear, or do I need to be more explicit?"

"Um."

"Well, your older listeners will know what I'm talking about, if they've followed me so far. The rest, I mean young people, they don't think, they don't have any brains nowadays. I mean, young people are shitheads. The older ones will get it.

"Dominique Rossi. Stand. Condom. AIDS. William Miller. They'll get it, they'll make the connection.

"Then *bam*, it'll all make sense. True love. Then hate. Then lies. Then the twist. With guys, that's just the way it goes."

36

Sundays, Will would go walking with friends in Buttes-Chaumont.

"A little nature can be cool."

That day Will was on his own. He went out in a dress, well made up, often with a dog. He liked to walk his friend Steven's rottweiler at nightfall. He went in concentric circles, then he'd take the little bridge, above the trees, then finally he'd climb up the hill to have a look at the view.

It was winter, and cold.

William didn't like being by himself. He felt fragile, tiny, and was given to anxiety attacks. So he walked quickly. The passersby looked at him, the couples, the families, the men on the benches; he walked with his head high. In these moments, William needed a man by his side, and he didn't have one. He looked at the city of Paris stretched out, already illuminated here and there with its houses lost to view beneath the darkening white sky, and his spirit sank: he felt as though he were surveying history itself. All those heroes, all those people who'd spent their time thinking, the whole mass of humanity who had simply *lived* and outweighed him in the balance, and all those civilizations too, for Christ's sake. History. As for him, he was just a poor faggot. All he asked was to have nothing to do with all that. But he would end up a poor crumb in this gigantic turd called History, completely indistinct from the rest. And then humanity would follow, humanity, who'd made all these houses out of stone, on the earth, and one day even the earth would explode. Fuck, there would be nothing left, and this gave him a headache.

"Motherfucker, I'm going to kill you."

At first he didn't understand—couldn't tell who was attacking him.

William lifted his hand to his face. It was the bone under his eye, but it seemed as though his eye itself were bleeding. He had scraped his knee on the gravel, and he hopped over toward the trunk of the nearest tree. There was no one in sight, the streetlights came on like a thousand paltry, regimented stars.

He lifted his head.

Doum grabbed him by the nape of his neck, punching him hard in the chest, over and over but with irregular blows.

William opened his eyes wide. Doum dragged him toward the fence. His dress was torn, and little trails of blood were running down his legs. He looked at the sky.

Doum thrust his head between the bars. Ouch! Will cried, the bars had torn the skin of his left ear. He was cold because of the metal, and Doum gave him a hard kick in the side. Trying clumsily to free himself, William cracked his jaw and split his lip against the black fence.

He was gasping for breath.

Doum tore at him. He was panting like a beast.

"Motherfucker, motherfucker."

With his fist Doum was hammering at the base of William's spine while he lay there in the flowerbed. He felt a bit like a princess in a fairy tale, dressed in her gown on a spring day, her forehead crowned with a wreath of a thousand flowers and a kiss.

Doum fractured William's skull, pounding it several times against the lamppost.

Dominique was beside himself. He roared. He wept.

William closed his eyes.

"That's so good . . ."

Doum couldn't stand it.

"You want to play with me? You want to provoke me, you little bitch?"

And he gave him two or three swift kicks in the balls. He jerked him up by the strap of his dress, which snapped.

Will had blood all over his face, one eye shut, a broken nose, a split lip, two teeth missing, his hair slick with blood, dirt, and saliva.

"My teeth! They don't hurt anymore!"

Doum was stunned. They faced each other, entirely hidden by the shadows of the trees. Dominique standing, fist closed, sniffling, William on his ass. There was a long silence between them.

Will brought his hand to his face, breathing hard. Dominique got out a cigarette and smoked it wordlessly.

Will closed his eyes again, he was happy, he wasn't alone.

Dominique trembled, he looked for something to say: the cigarette was finished before anything occurred to him. He tossed the butt at William's feet, William who lay stretched out, his dress torn, half conscious—and he left.

When he was by himself William felt the cold—and he realized that he hurt. He whimpered like a dog. He would have to wait for the night watchman to make his rounds.

He hurt terribly.

All around him the city was so big that you couldn't even see it anymore, and he was extremely afraid.

They took him to the hospital.

37

He went on with his promotional tour.

William walked onstage with his arm in a cast, his neck and jaw covered in bandages, stitches above his eye, ear swathed in gauze, supported by two young men, since it was said he couldn't really walk.

On TV programs, at this point, he'd always show up at the last minute. He demanded his own makeup artist, and he categorically refused to enter from backstage. That's only for the theater.

"Please, please help me welcome William Miller, who had the energy, the energy and the courage, to join us tonight."

It was a trendy cable show, the only one that broadcast live. It wasn't bad. I appeared sometimes as a special reporter.

As soon as he lifted one of his crutches, he tumbled over.

I hadn't heard from him in a while and, like many others, I was spending the evening alone in front of the TV.

The two kids came to pick him up. He slurred and seemed to be under the influence of something like morphine.

I started to feel for the host, who was already foundering.
"Hi."

"Hello there, William. It's good to have you back. But my God, what's happened to you?"

"'S nothing. I'm feeling great. Never better."

He tried to raise both crutches at once, to make a victory sign in the air, but he slid off the chair and crashed under the table. The two guys pushed the stagehands aside and lifted Will, who was chuckling, his eyes half closed.

"Right. Well, you ought to take better care of yourself, William. You've had a little fall."

"Huh, yeah, I opened the door and fell out, heh heh . . ."

"Yes, so, well, we haven't seen you since that business about, well, about what we might call the new practices—"

"Yeah, condoms."

"Right, right. You told us you were working on a new novel after the . . . um, disappointment of *My Friends Are My Enemies*, which—"

"My ma'terpiece."

"Yes, right, but which didn't exactly go . . . over . . ."

"People are retarded. 'S fucking genius."

"And . . ."

But it was over for the host. William could begin.

"Say, dickwad, really wanna know how this happened to me? I's attacked."

"Attacked?"

"By Arabs. 'S always the Arabs attacking Jews. Like Leibowitz said. I'm a Jew, remember?"

"Oh. Oh dear."

"No, no, I'm jus' fucking with you. I'm playing. I love the Arabs."

"Ah . . ."

"Them and their big hairy dicks. But no, seriously, I was a victim of faggot bashing. 'S fucked up."

He was like a science fiction teddy bear frozen in an artificial body; he smiled like an idiot, he couldn't turn his head and he had a bad cold, his nose was running and he couldn't wipe it.

He looked altogether beatific.

"Homophobes attacked me, they wanted to kill me. They called me a dirty faggot and they beat me up. I'm still in pain. The danger's everywhere, so are the homophobes—'s kind of like what Leibowitz says about the Arabs, who are always after the Jews. Don't know what this world is coming to, what with the homophobes and the anti-Semites. We're in trouble. We're fucked, just like he says."

The host, who'd had Leibowitz on two weeks before, tried to smooth things over, to protect Leibowitz, but Will was off and running.

"Homophobes, they're all Nazis! They tried to kill me, they want to kill all the Jews!"

And because he was moving around a little bit too much he fell out of his chair again.

The host took that moment to cut to a commercial.

When he came back, he looked utterly disconcerted.

Flanked by two security guys, who were themselves surrounded by the two gym rats, Will was ranting and refusing to leave the stage.

"I'm trying to tell you, I love the faggot bashers, you know why? Because I don't like faggot lovers. Faggot lovers like you. You people say, 'We like the little faggots,' except you don't even say 'faggots,' you say 'gays.' You want us to be part of society and have human rights like you because we're human beings like you. How fucking nice of you. But queers aren't human beings, we're extra-terrestrials. We're different, we're not like you. We don't want the faggot lovers' rights. They're all closet cases. They look and they don't touch. They say, 'We love you.' But if you love us, you have to fuck us. But the faggot bashers say, 'Death to the faggots.' And first off, at least they call us faggots, and tha's cool, thank you. Second off, they touch us, they mess us up, 's almost as if they fucked us. Personally, I like them. I say thank you. I like faggot bashers, they're real friends, and wha's more—"

They cut him off. The stage was in chaos.

That was the last time William really made a stir. The last time I saw him in a rectangle animated by points of light connected by an electric current that went out across the entire French territory and beyond. Television . . .

At the time I didn't care much one way or the other—and when I found out later what had actually happened, I saw it as a noble gesture, an old-fashioned chivalrous gesture, toward Dominique. Willie had said nothing against him. He wasn't a snitch.

He repaid goodness with badness, and vice versa, following no rule or law but his own whim, and really that must have been rooted in a kind of absolute fidelity—he was a good deal more faithful than others, at any rate.

JUSTICE

38

At first glance, the lawyer Malone agreed. There was a large so-cial question at stake.

He was born in 1952, at the same time—he liked to say—that Nasser seized power, to a father who was a notary and a mother who was a very rich Egyptian heiress. They lived in Provence. At the age of three Claude Malone accidentally set fire to his fa-ther's apartment, then took refuge on the balcony, where he was rescued by neighbors. A big man and a great seducer, silver-tongued and fond of cultivating, semi-ironically, his own legend, he liked to say, "My father must have realized I'd spend my life setting fires, then taking shelter while I watched them burn."

After ten years studying with the Jesuits, who taught him (as he said) cleverness and the importance of sex, a faithful Catho-lic, he began to practice law in the mid-seventies. He was close to the great Leclerc, a lawyer known far and wide for his human-ism, and for defending the rights of man in Homeric vitupera-tions. Malone made his name in Toulouse when he inherited a case of child murder in which he pleaded, against his client's wishes, that he be spared the death penalty.

Keeping faith with his mentor's ideals, almost lynched by the crowd as he left the courtroom, this aficionado of boxing, theater, and poetry got the first taste of his true love: the media. He had his rich clients and his paupers, as he put it, and thirteen attorneys on his staff. But he published a book every six months on history's great judicial errors or the scandal of the moment, and every talk show had a seat with his name on it.

And what was it all for?

William had met him on some kind of TV panel. Malone got along with everyone—there are no real friends in this milieu, he used to tell each of his friends, "except for you, *mon vieux*"—and they'd had an exchange of ideas on various topics: Malone was on the right, but of course he knew how to adapt.

He had an elegant wife and wore a large signet on his pinky, next to his wedding ring, with his family's coat of arms. He kept his watch on day and night ("Time never rests, *mon vieux*"). His hands had special importance to him. He was fat and didn't like to be reminded of the fact.

William asked him whether he was available to take a case— against Dominique, for poisoning with malice aforethought.

Malone sat down, switched off his cell phone, and thought it over.

"You mean he knew he had AIDS and had unprotected sex with you? We'd have to prove that it was him, that you didn't have sex with any other men."

He smiled and rubbed his neck.

"You know the saying: It takes just one photo to prove that you've cheated on your wife. To prove that you've been faithful is much more difficult. Some doubt always remains."

William was all enthusiasm.

"We could hire a private eye. We could reconstruct my daily activities, we could interview people, like in a Raymond Chandler novel! For three years I didn't sleep with anyone but him. Then he stopped being able to get it up—so it was trickier."

Malone sighed. They were sitting on a café terrace. He drank his beer.

"All right. It's doable. But complicated. It would be a very noisy affair. There's never been a conviction for giving someone AIDS. We'd have to attack the organization, I suppose. Let's see. There is definitely something here. It's complicated, but there's something."

William thwacked his fist, clumsily, into the palm of his hand.

"That's great, just great."

"Your first test?"

William frowned. "Mmm . . . It must have been"—he waved his hand vaguely—"around '97, I think."

"Positive?"

"Superpositive. Ultrapositive."

Malone put on his sunglasses. He thought some more.

"Well, we'll see."

"Cool. You know, I'm not doing it on principle. It's not for some universal principle. I couldn't give a fuck. I just want to get this guy. It's personal."

"OK. That's your business. But you'll have to keep that to yourself."

"And, well, I mean, it's also for money."

"Money! Now, see, that is going to cost you a pretty penny. If I take the case."

He took another sip.

"No, no. I mean, it's for me. I need money. I need to make something, because I'm kind of broke."

Malone didn't say anything, just sighed.

Willie jiggled his leg nervously. He scratched his beard. "And it's cool. I mean, even if I didn't tell you the truth, even if what I said is false, I could still win. For you it wouldn't change anything, right?"

"Well, it would change the means we used, but not the ends."

"Yeah, right, I was just saying. Because I'm sure it's true."

He took a pill with a glass of water.

"My friend, it isn't enough to be sure."

"Yeah, well, it *is* true. One hundred percent true."

Malone got up.

"Listen, really, this is going to cost you. So either you have the funds or else I'll give you the number of a colleague. A good one. Do you understand me?"

"What, are you fucking with me?"

Pitifully, Will decided to go ahead. On some level, he must have known he was sinking himself deeper and deeper.

But as long as he kept his head above water, he never doubted that he'd end up finding ground beneath his feet.

39

Dominique had had the chimney cleaned. The apartment smelled good and was warm. Out the bay window you could see part of the Cimiez Amphitheater, and the sky was blue, lightly streaked with white like very old stone.

He hadn't felt much need to redecorate. With time he discovered that he had more or less the same tastes as his father.

He was in slacks and a cardigan, a glass of port in his hand.

When he heard the bell he went to the door. It still stuck, a little. He'd have to grease the hinge.

He greeted Henri Vivier and invited him in.

The attorney, almost an old man now, bright-eyed, let his gaze wander over the grand salon, its parquet and its bookshelves beside the piano.

"You've cleaned the place up nicely. Ah, and you've got the chimney working."

"It wasn't hard. I had the chimney sweeps in. All they had to do was open the flue and give it a brush. Have a seat."

For a minute Vivier made polite small talk, then he came to the business at hand.

"Dominique, your father has left you the apartment and the house and the rest of it. I don't have to explain. He cared a great deal for you. You never came to see him."

Dominique scratched his ear, shamefaced, and bit at a piece of dry skin on his lower lip.

"I know. I do know. My brothers—"

Vivier put down his glass and sat back in the old armchair he knew so well.

"With Jean-Claude deceased, Damien is well set up in Brazil. He doesn't want for anything. The same is true of Nicolas, he has very happily signed his inheritance over to you. His business is going famously, he is a very generous and enterprising man . . ."

"When it suits him."

"José has taken the house in Tunisia, which was your father's wish. The largest share, he left to you. This was something he discussed with me. He loved you too much, you know that."

"Not really, no."

There was a heavy silence. The fire crackled, and beside the Palais Regina you could catch a glimpse of the soft rolling woods, the calm and open spaces of the slopes of Cimiez.

"Well. There are rumors going around in Paris, Dominique."

"I stopped following those some time ago."

"A lawyer named Malone, who is not exactly a friend, but who owes me a favor or two and knows I look after your interests, he . . . You must know there is the threat of a complaint being made against you. Out of motives that, well, I won't go into them here. But . . ."

Dominique stood and looked out the window at the town.

"Naturally, I wish to counterattack, Henri. Not out of—well, you must understand, it's not for personal reasons. There's a principle at stake. I have been confronted with someone who has plunged my life into blackness and is destroying me. But I'm not what matters here. What matters is his program, the evil he's spreading. Every day he destroys the lives of naïve young men, you know, who come up to Paris, running wild, without any idea that—well. It's a crime, what he does. I believe I have the means, the funds in any case, since Papa . . . I can see to it that he does no more harm. And that's why I asked you over, it's also because, you understand, I want to attack him and I want to be sure I'll win."

He turned.

Vivier held up a hand in warning. "As you know, one can never be sure of winning."

Dominique paced.

"What are my odds? What are my odds of attacking him, of making a complaint, and ruining him?"

"Oh, he's already ruined, I'd say. That's not the problem."

"What is the problem, then?"

"Your reputation. Your family. Your name. They're all gone. Under the circumstances, you have nothing to gain. You don't come from nowhere, Dominique—and this boy, he does, and soon he will disappear to where he came from. This is not a normal case. You can sue him, and I'll help you, obviously, but I want to make sure of your motives.

"Dominique, you have friends, and resources, and a name. You don't need a lawyer to tell you this. Thanks to your late father, you also have money. These are things no lawsuit, no trial can restore. On the contrary, these are precisely the things one must use to win in court.

"Think about it. And think of your father. I should go."

Dominique went to get his hat and coat. In the hallway he thanked him and shook his hand.

"Really, my boy, think it over."

When he'd pushed the door closed, Dominique returned to the window, where he watched the changing, vast sky and the verdant hill, in the heat of the wood fire, while Vivier, the old accomplice of his father, now dead and buried, picked his way toward the center of Nice along the boulevard de Cimiez and the boulevard Carabacel.

40

For several months Jean-Michel had been busy with a long inves-
tigative piece on the Muslim Brotherhood and their recent mu-
tation into "modernist democrats." In fact, it must be said, and
he said so himself, the true subject of the article was Hossan Hassam and his wife, in other words, the parents of Ali Hassam—in
other words, Ali Hassam.

Leibowitz considered Miller out of bounds because he was my
friend and because he was himself a Jew, whereas Miller's ex-
lover Ali, now an activist, a gadfly, a pro-Palestinian militant, and
the director of a gay rights organization, had become a total obsession for Leibo, who had decided to investigate him.

Ali's mother and father were all he talked about anymore. It
had become a sort of common noun at the table, on the phone,
in bed. Alismotherandfather.

In 1928 Hasan al-Banna founded Al-Jamiat al-Ikhwan al-
Muslimin, literally, the Society of Muslim Brothers. I am taking
my information from Leib's article, which isn't all that great a
source, but if you want better ones . . .

Well, I'm not going to read any more books for you, I've done
enough of that already.

Leibowitz analyzed the Brotherhood's role, the actions of its
Palestinian branch, in the insurrection of 1936. Palestine had
always been a structural axis of the Brotherhood.

In 1945, at the end of the war, Said Ramadan created the Palestinian equivalent of the movement and fought in 1948 against the soldiers of the brand-new Israeli state.

In 1948 the Muslim Brotherhood killed the Egyptian prime minister; al-Banna was assassinated in reprisal and, in 1951, the organization was dissolved. Under Nasser, who advocated a pan-Arabism based on Arab, rather than Islamic, unity, twenty thousand militants found themselves behind bars. To one degree or another, Sadat and Mubarak both used the Brotherhood for their own political ends.

In 1982, in Syria, Hafiz al-Assad suppressed Al-Talia al-Muqatila, the Botherhood's armed vanguard. Deformed by a long irreversible slide toward dictatorship on the part of those who represented the hopes of Arab nationalism and decolonization, the organization was to change, grow, and swell the opposition, so that gradually it fomented a resistance movement, enjoying an aura of legitimacy in its fight against the secretive and corrupt Middle Eastern governments and, on a global scale, against the United States.

That, explains Leibowitz, is when things got interesting. Hossan Hassam, a medical student sent on a mission to Syria, fled the country—enraging Assad, who sent his secret service after him. In Syria, Hossan had met his wife, Heba Kanaan, the daughter of a powerful Alaouite family who had often crossed paths with Assad.

According to Leibowitz this alliance, between a traitress to one of the most powerful and richest Syrian families and a man of seemingly liberal ideas, now working as a pharmacist (like many other militants of the Middle East since the war in Algeria), made these two a symptomatic couple. Hossan, who went back to Cairo and helped overthrow the old guard of the Muslim Brotherhood in the early '90s, was also the author of scholarly, virulently anti-Israeli texts. He combined an unbending respect for traditions that, to Western eyes, seemed archaic with a modernist discourse adapted to the struggles of the twenty-first century. This man with his short neat beard and Western clothes, who spoke fluent English, German, French, and Italian and was close to Makran al-Devri, this was Ali's father. They had Ali in 1981. In Cairo he attended an excellent school in Zamalek, then was sent to boarding school in London.

In 1996, while he helped to found Al-Wasat, the party that revived the Brotherhood, Hossan argued quietly, as a member of the rank and file, in favor of democratic elections and a platform adapted to contemporary realities, albeit firmly grounded in the past. Leibowitz thought he might have been part of the move to replace the Brotherhood's old symbol—two crossed sabers—with a clod of earth, held in two hands, from which a seed is sprouting.

By part two of his "journalistic" exposé, Leibowitz was already highlighting the ambiguities in the various speeches given by Hossan, who had been in hiding since 1997, when his party was banned. He dug up one text in particular, *The Sanctioned and the Forbidden: Living a Religious Life Today*, which echoed the positions of Hossan's alleged friend Youssef Qaradhaoui, citing traditional Islamic teachings on homosexuality: "Legal scholars could never agree on the punishment . . . Should the active partner be put to death or the passive partner? By what means? . . . This severity, which may strike us as inhumane, was simply a way to purify Islamic society from those harmful entities that lead inevitably to a loss of humanity." Hossan Hassam himself defined homosexuality as an imbalance, and according to Leibowitz, whom I entirely believed, he was—beneath his pro-democracy veneer—an obscurantist whose thinking began and ended with his driving hatred for Israel, the vanguard of the Americanized West; in its turn, this hatred subsumed his disgust with the states of the Middle East, rich with promise in the sixties, which had become, with the consent and paternalistic support of the West, dictatorships favoring one class, one ultrawealthy and corrupt family, materially and spiritually exploiting those who had no education.

The problem arose at the end of Part Four. Leibo got more and more sidetracked by Ali, Hossan's son, who had gone off to London and then apparently taken refuge in Paris in 1998, even before the 2001 roundup of fifty-two "presumed" homosexuals at the *Queen Boat* nightclub, moored on the Nile. Although he did not have papers, he was rather mysteriously welcomed into the country, aided and abetted by William Miller, who'd helped him get papers. Leibowitz himself (thanks to me) had, in a grumbling concession to "left-wing generosity," supported the young Egyptian's visa application during the movement to regularize illegal aliens in France. He was very clear about it, and quite bitter too. It was one of his regrets.

What had Ali been up to since then? Spreading Palestinian propaganda on French soil, said Leibo. Claiming to have broken with his parents, "as do all young immigrants to our shores" (this was the first point of his polemic), he benefited from French hospitality in order to stab Israel in the back.

Leibowitz's thesis, which he expressed well—and which, if you asked me to sum up his character, synthesized his whole life and work—was that we never escape our parents, we are our parents' trustees and representatives for all time.

And so, Leibo concluded, given Ali Hassam's parents, no one should be surprised by what was starting to appear: a new kind of anti-Semite, a modern anti-Semite. A left-wing schizophrenic for our times, who, victimized by his parents' homophobia, became a persecutor of Jews.

He ended—and made the second point of his polemic—with this description: "A 'faggot,' the son of homophobes, and to keep faith with his ancestors whom he had betrayed, an anti-Semite. As for Miller, the son of Jews . . ."

What a disaster. Poor Leibo.

Where to begin?

There was the word *faggot* and the quotation marks. People argued a lot about those quotation marks. Leibowitz, on Europe 1, declared: "Everybody knows that, ever since Stonewall and the rest of it, the homosexual community has made a practice of reclaiming the insults used against it. Ali Hassam, and I have quotations to this effect, uses the word to describe himself. In this interview right here he says, 'As a faggot, I' et cetera. Furthermore, I put the word in quotation marks, so why shouldn't I describe him by the very word he uses to describe himself?"

"But you are not a homosexual, are you, M. Leibowitz?"

"No, I'm not. So? Do we use different words to designate a certain quality, depending whether we possess that quality or not? You see, it's exactly this schizophrenia that I was trying—"

You get the idea. Soon Leib was pilloried for his insults to Ali's family, and then Ali issued his own response.

According to him, he couldn't stand the atmosphere in Egypt in '98 or the arrest of all those young men, some of whom he knew personally, on charges of "Satanism." When he was supposed to go back to London, feeling unable to tell his father the truth, he decided instead to go to Paris. He never saw his father again.

"What M. Leibowitz doesn't understand is that I hate my parents, that I'm nothing like them, and that I oppose what they do. No, I am not some horrible representative of theirs, or some kind of Trojan horse for the Muslim Brotherhood. If you ask me, they're fascists, and I certainly don't need my parents' help to believe that today's Palestinians have the right to a state, and that the UN's resolutions have never been respected by that other state whose name M. Leibowitz is fond of repeating."

Leibowitz fought back on France Info, calling Ali a negator of Israel, which only made things worse.

And then there was the chiasmus.

Ali was the one who noticed it. Leibo had called him a faggot, the son of homophobes, then called Miller a son of Jews,
therefore—therefore what? Logically, Ali remarked—in *Libération*, in an op-ed approved by Doumé's replacement, Raphael—if
homophobe is the opposite of *faggot* then the opposite of *Jew* is . . .
Nazi. Leibowitz had *explicitly* called William a Nazi through a
chiastic figure of speech.

The Chiasmus Debate turned into a regular brawl.

Leibowitz didn't really see why everyone misunderstood him:
"Ali's just a pawn. Someone behind him has it in for me."

Leibowitz didn't understand why people didn't get it—that
we all come from our parents. Or as he put it at the height of the
affair: we are our parents. We can accept them, we can reject
them. Either way, we *are* them. He emphasized the word with a
smug pout reminiscent of Lacan, whose seminar he had taken
with Dominique those many years ago.

Then, after a silence: "Look at *me*."

I did what I could to support Leibowitz during the controversy. He was hated. His parents didn't understand. I could have,
I should have left him then, but not when he was in trouble. For
better and for worse—it doesn't matter that he never said the
words, or that I didn't, either.

He couldn't sleep. He said he'd been "thrown to the PC dogs."

He consulted his friend Vivier. The lawyer.

"You've certainly put your foot in it, Jean-Michel."

Ali didn't prosecute the case on his own behalf. No, in the
name of Stand and the old association known as CRAC—
Contre le Racisme et l'Amnésie Coloniale, formerly Contre le
Racisme, l'Antisémitisme et la Censure—he brought a complaint
of racism against Leibo on the grounds of a suggestive ellipsis.

Vivier, who had just come back from Nice, explained to Leib:
"The trouble is that rhetorical figure. It's a chiasmus, or really
it's an analogy that turns on a chiasmus: between the word

homophobes and those three dots there must be the same relation that there is between the words *faggot* and *Jew*, both of which are inverted. Since you call Ali's parents homophobes whose son is a faggot, so in Miller's case, since his parents are Jews, it stands to reason that the equivalent of *faggot*, in quotes, and of the son, must stand in the same relation to *Jew* that *homophobe* stands in relation to, quote, *faggot*. In other words, Nazi. It's unanswerable."

Leibowitz in his velvet armchair, surrounded by his philosophy books, shook his head. "No, no. You don't understand. Nobody understands. I put that ellipsis in there specifically because it's not a chiasmus and I certainly wasn't calling Miller a, quote, Nazi. Besides, the word never once appears. That's what's so crazy, I never said it. What I wrote is a sentence fragment in the conditional! And I only meant to say that Miller, too, is a, quote, faggot while being the son of Jews, while Ali is a, quote, faggot, while being the son of homophobes. You know what it is? It's an *asymmetrical* chiasmus! But nobody seems able to get that through their heads . . ."

"Indeed." Vivier consulted his pocket watch. "My dear Leibowitz, what we have here is a problem of rhetoric. From that angle it will be very hard to defend you. People simply won't understand anything quite so gnomic. I'm telling you this as your counsel and an experienced attorney. You need to be more forceful, you need to take a stand, to take the plunge."

"I was trying to throw the reader off by taking the other side."

"Yes, the other side, but that's just what people won't understand."

Vivier was quick to finish his coffee.

Leibowitz was aghast. All this fuss over Miller. He had bags under his eyes and he'd grown more and more clumsy.

He tried to make light of it.

"You know, when we were at the École Normale with Rossi . . . There was Althusser. This was before the business with Hélène—

with his wife. My God, I can just see him in his office, the old crocodile, talking to me about Derrida—and you know, this was when Derrida meant something—saying how Derrida could do a triple dialectical somersault in the air, saying the opposite of what he said, then the opposite of that, and land on his feet. 'It's more than philosophy,' Althusser told me, 'it's gymnastics.' "

"And you, my friend," said Vivier, rising to his feet, "have made a wobbly landing. That's the trouble. It's always the trouble for intellectuals, coming back down to earth after they've turned a phrase."

Leibowitz thought for a moment. "What does Rossi say? Have you seen him?"

"Oh, he has difficulties of his own."

Leibowitz sighed; the world had risen up against him. The revelations in Willie's book, which had put a considerable strain on our relationship, had also hurt the author of *Fidelity for Life*. He'd lost much of his support. The rug had been pulled out from under him. People said he'd slipped up one time too many.

"They still support me in Israel."

At the door, Vivier nodded. "I should hope so."

"At least the Israeli left respects me." Leibowitz tsked. "I've had enough of these intellectual games. I'm sick of it. Utterly sick."

"You need to think hard about your defense," said Vivier on his way out. "All I can do is advise you. Ali Hassam will have retained Malone. Malone knows you. It could be messy."

With that he waved goodbye.

A week or two after it was all over, Leibowitz's father died.

HAPPINESS

41

Entranced, Willie walked down Ben Yehuda Street and rested, for a moment, on Zion Square. Barefoot on the pavement, in his T-shirt and sunglasses, he watched the people drift in and out of the pedestrian mall.

Trees in cubical wooden planters, spaced at intervals, provided shade from the hot afternoon, between the two rows of sandy-colored buildings, their doors and windows often half hidden behind white shades. A banner stretched high above the street, three red circles, one white one. As far as the eye could see, men wandered across the terrace of a café, some in yarmulkes, some bareheaded, amid the plastic chairs. We aren't far from the center of the world, Willie thought. There was something overwhelming about it. The houses, all this accumulation, and history. But then that was Jerusalem.

The shops were all open, a very delicate arcade sheltered a group of girls in slacks, and the sky was blue. The sky, which seemed less important than the city.

Oh, Willie thought, these are human beings. And he felt completely overwhelmed.

He had always wanted to get back to his Jewish roots. Not the religion so much, more the city.

It was different from in the United States. In New York, in San Francisco, he'd found a city that included him, a city where he belonged. And the community. But then he'd ended up at odds with all those Americans, all the ones he knew. They were too much. Too futuristic, in the end.

Jerusalem was beyond passé. He felt that, to be part of it, he'd have had to be a stone. And it had always seemed to him that, in one way or another, he didn't exist any more or less than a stone. And he felt asexual in Jerusalem.

His publisher, Claude, had come up with a little plan, a trip, a conference, two or three meetings. Miller wasn't working anymore in France, so this was also a way of getting rid of him, if only for the moment . . . With him you never knew. Maybe he'd have an epiphany, maybe he'd convert and stay in the Holy Land forever.

Why not?

It was the light.

If only he'd been a painter, for this city. It made him wish he had been an artist, made him feel like being a writer. Because he was one—but not really, he'd never had any illusions on that score.

He meditated, like Spinoza.

He already had very little left. He smiled. Could I have somehow become wise, to be content with so little? I don't need a lover, or love. By himself he strolled in the city, a knapsack on his back, hands in his pockets. Until nightfall. He blew off all his appointments.

He loved Israel very much, and he felt like an adult, he felt old, he felt like stone.

The world is so full of things I don't know, and I was always so busy being me, hardly anything, a little stone.

I suppose that on Ben Yehuda Street, a stranger in old Jerusalem, under the big sun, William Miller, little Willie, who had left Amiens so long ago, said to himself in one way or another: Well, it's over. One must know how to end things, not to hang on

forever, and all these stone cities, all these people's houses, all
this history, all of this will go on existing. And that's how it
should be. It's cool. I think he must have smiled. It's odd to imagine Will a grown-up and at peace. At peace in Jerusalem.

It had to end, of course. Will did what he always did, and
that's what people talked about back in France. Not about some
walk he took down Ben Yehuda Street . . .

Invited to the LGBTQ Community Center on this street,
right there, where the rainbow flag was floating in the breeze, he
gave a talk on the state of the French queer community. With a
benign smile he attempted to describe the character of Dominique Rossi to the handful of gay intellectuals in attendance—
and he'd had to do a good job, since these were potential converts.
He painted Dominique Rossi's portrait as a homosexual leader
who was profoundly anti-Semitic. People took notes, nodding.
Hardly surprising, given the recent developments in France.

Then, after one night in a hotel, his publisher had arranged
for him to meet with two reporters from the cultural page of
Haaretz. William explained to Yitzchak Ratner and David Shen-
hav that Leibowitz, a person well known there among the Jewish left, was being prosecuted in France—as a terrible Jewish
homophobe—and he cited the current controversy.

Leibowitz was friendly with Amira Mass, a journalist from
Haaretz who, because she supported the Palestinian cause, was
considered a traitor by some. *Haaretz* readers often canceled
their subscriptions over her muckraking reports. In the tight-knit
world of Israeli intellectuals, there were heated arguments over
Leibowitz as a person and over his objective role in France. William
was pleased to sow the seeds of his destruction, and in the eyes of
his old supporters in faraway Israel, Leibowitz began to seem, at the
height of the affair, at the very least an ambiguous character.

This is all William ever told me about his trip across the
Mediterranean:

"I liked the idea of leaving behind something of myself, somewhere that wasn't Paris."

"Shit?" I suggested. "Discord? Hatred?"

He smiled. "They've already got that. No, why not? I enjoyed it. As long as it was mine. As long as it was there. When I'm not around anymore. All those stones, on that land and that street, underneath the sky. If you think how many streets there are, and how many stones, on this planet, each one different from the others, underneath the same sun . . ."

He paused.

"And all those suns, in the universe, which is so huge. And just one you. Maybe Spinoza was wrong."

He'd done his thing over there, chipping away at Dominique and the Leib. That was just for the sake of fighting on, of going on in the same spirit. He didn't actually have much hope of winning.

I still imagine William happy on Ben Yehuda Street, astonished by the flagstones, the trees, the buildings, the people. I think the existence of something outside himself—the existence of people, of the world—always came as a kind of revelation, for ever since he was little, and in all his daily life, he had trouble believing for more than a second in the existence of anything outside himself and, my God, it's not as if he had lived less than others, in his way. He was no less a man than anyone else. At any given moment he might have grasped, might have understood that yes, all that existed, just the way he did.

And I like to think this was the case on Ben Yehuda Street.

AT PEACE WITH
THE PAST

42

They met at Bouillon Racine, on the corner of boulevard Saint-Michel.

Dominique stood and greeted Jean-Michel. This first contact was extremely chilly.

"Hello, Rossi."

"Hello, Jean-Michel."

They sat beside the staircase, and the waiter interrupted their first silence by offering them the wine list.

"You used to like the rosé, no?"

Jean-Michel grunted.

They didn't begin to speak until the food arrived.

Dominique put down his fork and apologized.

"Forgive me, Jean-Michel."

Leibowitz swallowed his wine. His hand fell hesitantly to his bread, then he made a gesture, a little tap of the fingertips on the checkered tablecloth, which meant: "It's nothing, Rossi. It was years ago, let's forget all about it. I was as much in the wrong as you."

Which is more or less what he said.

Dominique asked after Sara's health. She was well—I, obviously, was not a topic of conversation. And the children, they were about to be eighteen and sixteen. Soon it would be the end for them, or rather the beginning. And they were beautiful kids.

Leibowitz smiled. He mentioned his father. "What can you do, that's life. But all that heartache, it killed him. It really did."

Jean-Michel ventured a few words about Dominique's father. Dominique was touched. "Nothing is worse than losing your parents, Rossi. We're orphans."

Pushing the bread across his plate, he reminded Dominique of the time when his father had come to Paris to see his son. Jean-Michel had joined them for dinner, which ended badly because of politics.

"Can you believe how we used to browbeat each other over the future of the Programme Commun back then? What idiots we were."

They talked about Elias, the terrible Elias—now dead for two years and almost entirely forgotten. What had happened to him?

They discussed their old friends.

Leibowitz smiled. "I think it was Alain who said, 'I'll write you an e-mail,' it was for that conference on peace in the Middle East, and I said, 'Alain, I don't know how to use it,' and he said he wasn't surprised, but how on earth did I manage to survive?"

Dominique shrugged. "I've lost interest. You see how the gay community's imploded, thanks to the Web. It's rotted away from within. The problem, of course, is that no one can come out and say it."

"You know, this idea of being connected . . . Ah la la." Then Leibowitz burst out laughing. "Aren't we a couple of old fucks?"

Dominique was laughing too. "You said it. Two old fucks."

"Cigarette?"

"I wouldn't say no."

They smoked.

Dominique coughed and spread his hands on the table. "Well, I don't imagine we're here for no reason."

"No, of course not. Though it feels natural, doesn't it?"

Leibowitz was in deep trouble. In his personal life, Sara had told him he had to choose between her and me—and of course there was this complaint of Ali's hanging over his head, accusing him of hate speech. Since he had already contested the law against hate speech some years before, it was uncomfortable to find himself up against it now. They didn't like him much anymore in Israel. William had dragged him through the mud. He needed help. He'd hit bottom.

Dominique presented his side of the question. He was nobody now. The community no longer really existed, or else it had forgotten about him. Rumor had it that he was not just a hypocrite but a bastard, that he'd deliberately infected that shit Miller. Even so, he still had a few sympathizers on the left. He had money.

Dominique explained that he didn't want anything for himself, he was ready to put everything on the table for one principled reason: to ensure that people stop talking about Miller.

Leibowitz made it clear that he had nothing in particular against Miller, that he understood Dominique, that he hated Ali, and that he wanted to be done with this mess and regain a certain visibility.

"Roughly speaking, I've got the paper, I mean *Le Figaro*, the right, a big chunk of the establishment—but no new media, no intellectuals, and none of the do-gooders. That's roughly speaking."

Dominique sipped his coffee. "I see what you mean. I have my paper, *Libération*, some goodwill with the Old Left, some connections in the prevention movement and the ministry, and I can get back some of the more chastened elements of the community—but that's it."

They looked at each other and chuckled.

"Well, it's a little bit complicated, but we're from the same world. It's as simple as that. I need you and you need me. We have all we need, if you get right down to it, all we need to do is muster our resources. This Miller . . . Miller's nothing."

"It's true. Nothing."

They fought over the check.

"All right, why don't you pay mine and I'll pay yours."

How happy they must have been to be reunited. They talked about their old teachers, they talked about literature, they left politics alone.

They went to the Compagnie bookstore.

It was a cold, dry day.

Dominique buttoned up his long black coat, and Leibowitz gazed at the bare branches of the trees.

"It's strange how long it takes to figure out where you belong, where you're at home . . ."

"Can I offer you a cigarillo?"

Leibowitz grinned. "All we need to do is strike, like conspirators. Do you remember the time we ran into those Trotskyites, in rue Saint-Jacques?"

Dominique burst into a raucous laugh. He had stopped coughing. "It's true, all we need to do is strike."

And into the bookstore they went.

43

It turned out to be quite a success. As the reporter from *Le Nou-vel Observateur* put it, each absolved the other in plain view.

A Generation Looks Back, published by Fayard, was basically a series of interviews between Dominique Rossi and Jean-Michel Leibowitz, on communism, the left, anti-Semitism, the homosexual community, the conflicts in the Middle East, France today, and their own lives.

Of course you will guess that, if I'm writing this today, it's because nothing in the book—although it was by no means dishonest—reflected any of what you've read so far.

So Dominique Rossi was presented as the founder of Stand, the leading figure of AIDS prevention in France, a culture journalist for *Libération*, and a member of the Ethics Committee of the Socialist Party (which was news to me). None of it was false, obviously, but it didn't include much of the truth—of the real truth, anyway.

For his part, Jean-Michel Leibowitz was a writer and philosopher, a teacher of political science; as everybody knew, a chevalier of the Legion of Honor, the author of numerous works including *Fidelity for Life*, and a leading columnist for *Le Figaro*. His other books included *The Failure of Intellect, the Intellect of Failure*. Married for twenty-five years. Two children. Fuck it. To think that for many people (not you), who'll spend twenty-two euros for this (fat) book, they will be *that*. You know better.

So they staged their debate. It was an exercise in self-criticism. The book sized up their careers and mistakes, which they acknowledged "without the vainglory of believing they couldn't be helped, without the shame of believing they could have been entirely avoided." It was fine writing.

The book revolved around one man whose name—unless I am mistaken and the index is incomplete—was never spoken. You know who I mean.

Dominique, who sketched the meaning of his struggle and the long march accomplished by the gay community, paradoxically saw its victory as its dilution, its integration into society: "The community has sometimes been ungrateful to its key supporters, because their success has brought about a progressive assimilation into the social body. Personally, I consider that an achievement. There are so many things we don't have to fight for nowadays."

Leibowitz asked him about the resistance of those who clung to a mythical, fanatical idea of homosexuality as an "absolute difference." Dominique brushed them aside. Having come late to the battle, they'd gone about inventing themselves a war.

And Dominique questioned Leibowitz about the end of the left, the preservation of Jewish identity, communitarianism, the infighting nature of French society. Here too, it was time to deal squarely with what had been gained, and what had been lost.

Dominique acknowledged some sectarian missteps in his early activism, Leibowitz looked back unsparingly on his too hasty reversals of opinion, his overly theoretical bent, his polemics where they might have wounded innocent people of good faith and where, thanks to him, their feelings of community might have been bruised.

It wasn't that the book was bad, no, the trouble was that it was a success. Rossi went back on television, where he was now rather more at ease. Leibowitz grew a little beard, and he came back to shake hands with his old Socialist friends. Former gay militants, old leftists, socialists, or right-wing columnists all felt melancholically absolved and accepted by the center.

Those who criticized the book seemed extreme. That was the whole point. In the last chapters, devoted to the "Barbarians of the Dream," the figure of the "radical," who'd haunted the book throughout, was depicted as an enfant terrible who would never grow up and never take responsibility for anything, unable to respect his adversary and unable to accept the existence of other people. Using barebacking as an example, Dominique denounced the vice inherent in the dream of freedom, the denial of reality, and the childish titillation with death. Later on these guys understand how stupid they've been and they come crying to the organizations, but it's too late, and the ones who'd held out the prospect of an absurd pleasure are no longer around, they've dropped them and gone off in search of fresh blood.

Leibowitz agreed and went on to describe the Irresponsible Man as one who denied the existence of the Other because he couldn't accept the idea that he was himself the other in the eyes of somebody else, in the eyes of society.

The book saw in the left a crisis of ideals, an enraged impulse to consider the world as subject to the individual will, subject to an adolescent rejection of father figures—and Leibowitz saw in the figure of the Irresponsible Man one who, as the son of the Sons, tried to mimic their rebellion and, rebelling against rebels, turned his back on society, that battlefield of the generation of '68, in order to create a "negative rebellion" of the individual, denying his fellow man and turning the fathers' own concepts against them, concepts once full of meaning, now empty: Nazi, victim, ideology, repression, freedom . . . All of which led him into absurdity.

Published in early September, at the height of the publishing season, the lavishly illustrated book sold briskly among the middle classes, the veins of society, and flowed into the media, accompanied by the regular celebratory drumbeat of the intellectuals, journalists, and reviewers who recognized themselves in the book, or pretended they did.

The headline in *L'Express* read "A Generation Reunited." The Family, after so many ruptures, now looked back with a nostalgic, clear, and kindly eye on its past.

And those who didn't belong . . .

Well, it's a tautology! They were excluded.

They could see the door, but they were missing the key.

44

When Dominique saw Jean-Michel, he burst out laughing. "Don't tell me I have to wear a suit!"

Jean-Michel looked sheepish. He was wearing a white shirt and a tight black jacket, and he smiled. "We don't have to match."

And then they went out on stage.

The Théâtre du Rond-Point drew a mixed crowd. But tonight, mainly men between the ages of thirty-five and fifty. They applauded.

The title of the talk was "Where Does AIDS Come From?"

The debate was the finale of Dominique and Jean-Michel's book tour. The spectators sat chin in hand, nearly all in neatly pressed shirts.

"This is a provocative question, naturally . . ."

Dominique brought the microphone closer and explained, "We haven't completely lost it, after all."

Half the audience laughed. The other half applauded.

Someone sitting in the back of the house, to their left, called out, "Don't worry, you're among friends."

Leibowitz leaned over the table, spread his arms, and pushed aside the glass of water. "We're not going to talk tonight about the science per se, or the material origins of AIDS as a disease—we want to understand the phenomenon as it erupted in the realm of ideas . . . How this terrible disease became a sort of wager, a piece of intellectual blackmail, or a vector of hysterias from all sides. The time has come to lay it all out. Personally, I am quite ready to question my own positions, which have tended to stigmatize the more enlightened militants, those who have been fighting for life, such as Dominique Rossi, who will take a hard look at his own years in the struggle. Obviously there are those who, even now, still refuse to take up the work of self-criticism . . ."

Laughter, fidgets.

"We'll get to that." He turned toward Dominique. "Bearing in mind, of course, what is most immediate, concrete, and cruel about the disease itself. Dominique knows all too well, I'm sorry to say, since he lives with this threat every day."

Applause. What could one say? This was only common sense. He shook his head. One couldn't let such a thing happen.

And when Dominique said, "As we know, it's a phenomenon with two faces, like Janus, one natural, the other inherently political. There's no need to go back to 1872, or to Kaposi, we must know how to acknowledge this natural aspect, we may not have done enough, in the beginning, which is a key moment for scientific research to . . ."

Someone stood up shouting, pointing toward the stage. There were five others with him, they'd taken off their coats to show their T-shirts: "Prevention=Repression, DR+JML= Mental AIDS."

Dominique blanched, Jean-Michel crossed his arms and said nothing. He leaned toward Dominique, whispering, "The game's up, don't worry. This is just what we wanted."

And he gestured calmly toward the agitators who stood with their arms raised at the back of the hall, and toward the one who brandished his fist and shouted at the audience. People had turned in their seats, whispering and uneasy.

"We have nothing to say, and yet you censure us, you tell us to roll over and get in line behind the Party, behind all the paternalist institutions. I'll tell you what you want. You want all faggots dead, you want there to be no more faggots, you want the extinction of the race, the word, and the reality."

He held up a ridiculous little sign: "Freedom of Expression, Freedom of Ejaculation."

"You tell us to wait like good little boys, to be careful and responsible." He pointed toward a prevention poster: "Take Responsibility."

"But who are you?" The more he went on, the louder he shouted, and the more the audience groaned.

The security guards were taking their time.

Dominique leaned toward Leibowitz. "He's reciting one of my speeches, from the eighties, you know, from outside Socialist headquarters."

Jean-Michel nodded. "It's completely out of context. It's over."

"We have the right to love, and you have the duty to save us."

The audience was shocked. They booed, and the intruders found themselves bundled out into the lobby.

When it was over, Daniel, who'd been reinstated as a Socialist deputy, came up to shake hands with Dominique and Jean-Michel.

"Good to see you."

"And you, comrade." They remembered the old days, the green corridor on the second floor, and they laughed at the memories.

Dominique tugged at his earlobe: "That was him. He came to give one of my old speeches. You know, that's what I said in rue Solferino. The rally with the gaffer tape." He laid a finger to his lips, meaning quiet.

"Oh, yeah. That's true. Well, back then it made sense."

Jean-Michel finished his water, surrounded by the buzz of guests.

"That's always been his m.o., in one way or another. He throws that in our faces, as if we were betraying something, when in fact we've changed. Everything around us has changed. Not him. The same speech isn't the same speech twenty years later. I don't see why he doesn't get it."

I heard him say that—I was adjusting the shawl on my bare shoulders—two meters from the other side of the buffet.

Daniel polished his glasses and asked Dominique, "What about the community? Who does it support? Him? Or has it come around to your side, now that everyone's older?"

Dominique helped himself to another glass. "The community doesn't exist. Everyone over thirty agrees with us, because we're right. The ones who want to be wrong, they don't think, they have their fun, they're scattered here and there, they don't represent anything anymore."

Daniel twisted his lips. "Well, too bad for them."

And they went off to say hello to Alexandre, a prefect and former comrade, and his wife and a couple of others.

I looked down at my dress, which didn't look as bad as all that, and I had a third glass of wine, and I stood where I was, because I didn't know anybody there.

SEPARATIONS

45

I was leaving the pool around two. I'd dried my hair—it was short now. The swimming pool was empty on the other side of the glass, and the water was peaceful, transparent all the way to the bottom of this cube, which from far away looked like a yellow and green aquarium. I turned my cell phone on.

I was already hurrying down the street, flushed, shivering from the cold.

I wasn't expecting it.

"Can you come over? Elizabeth?"

I went. He named a hotel near the Gare du Nord. Not very nice. A slab of grayish brown building, a yellowing white sign. I pinched my nose. My fingers smelled of chlorine. I felt dizzy, my heart contracting.

He was staying in the annex, across the courtyard, past the little landing for rooms 27, 28, and 29. Some sheet metal and an oil drum cluttered the path to his door, which was paneled with smoked glass.

As I knocked, my gaze wandered to the piss-colored carpet. I hadn't even seen a desk clerk.

"It's me."

"Who do you mean?"

"It's me."

"Who?"

"Elizabeth."

He opened the door. His lower jaw seemed to jut out, which it never had. His toothache had deformed his face.

The place stank. Of meat.

"I bought myself a pork chop. Mind if I finish?"

"OK."

I looked for somewhere to sit, and found a wicker-bottomed chair. I didn't take off my fur coat. I kept my handbag in my lap.

"You eat meat now."

He nodded. "Constantly. It's good for the blood. Guys who don't eat meat"—swallowed a mouthful—"can't get it up. Like Dominique. They haven't got the blood. Plus it's for the disease. It makes you stronger."

I let this go.

"See, a dick's like a sponge, so you need lots of blood for it to get hard. The blood's important." And he pushed his fork into the miserable dry bit of pork until a tiny drop of juice oozed onto the paper plate. He sopped it up with his bread. He didn't say anything more.

I smoked. After ten minutes went by and I'd taken in the windowpane, the dim light, the single bed with its white sheets, the blank TV, and the half-open door to the toilet, I said, "Will, why did you ask me here?"

He stared at me in confusion.

He looked so . . . finished. So sad. His jaw, his eyebrows. I couldn't help asking, "Are you all alone here, Will?"

He wiped his face nervously with a tissue.

"No, not at all. I'm fine. I have lots of friends. I've got a plan."

So I understood.

I'm not the crying kind—not when it's really sad.

I sighed.

He smiled, proud of himself. His teeth were yellow, the lower half of his face was twisted.

"It's cool, I mean, can't you sometimes see old friends?"

Then he sped up his delivery, jiggling his right leg.

"I've got it all figured out, Liz. I've got a plan."

I was leaving the culture section, at the paper. They'd made me an editor.

He beat around the bush, then awkwardly he spat it out:

"I think I—do you want to interview me?"

"I don't do that anymore, Will."

I was ready to stay there all afternoon, doing nothing, just sitting there. I, who was supposed to be so jealous of my time. Here I was seeing an old friend.

"Come on, I have a tape recorder right here, if you want. It's a plan, it's a good plan. You interview me, you know, you interview me, and . . . and it comes out great! Wait, wait—here it is. Give it a try."

I turned the tape recorder over in my hands, my heels deep in the staticky carpet.

"The thing is, Liz, I need to get published."

I sniffed. "I love you, Will. You know that. I'll do whatever you want. But I can't promise anything."

"You know, Liz"—he winked—"publish or perish."

He was acting like a little kid.

"So, you know, you be the journalist. Like that. Now you ask me some questions, softballs." He imitated me. "You know, like 'Good morning, M. Miller, what brings us together to-day?' "

I sighed.

"And then I answer. I've got stuff, lots of stuff, to say. I haven't got time to write it all down, though. You need to interview me."

"What's this plan of yours, Will?"

He straightened up, he wiped his lips, very proud. For a second I could still believe in him.

"I'm going to tell my life story. We're going to turn it into a book, you and me."

I looked at the tape recorder.

"A book . . . like Doum and Leibo. But that's the thing. I have so much stuff to talk about. So do you. It'll be a hit, we'll make a killing, and then I can destroy them. If I can just get the cash together, there's this lawyer I know, he's ready to help me, and we're going to let them have it. I prove Dominique's the one who gave me the virus, see, and you, you take the money and you can destroy Leibowitz, if you want. Hear me? You can destroy him."

"Oh, Will. I don't want to destroy him."

"Really? Well, OK. But . . ."

"Will, we've got nothing to say. We can't make a book. You, me, we're not like them. We're not part of the same thing. We don't even have the same past. It doesn't make any sense."

"Yes, it does. You're being defeatist, Liz. Hold on. I have these revelations, lots of them. Hold on, listen to what Dominique told me this one time . . ."

He pressed the ON button of the recorder. "He told me"—now the tape started to turn, as he imitated Dominique—"The Jews are the ones who invented AIDS. It was the Jews, those fucking shitbags, who invented AIDS in their laboratories after the Yom Kippur War. It was a biological weapon. That's the truth, there's proof."

I turned it off. "Cut it out, Willie. You're talking nonsense. You need to sort this out."

"Oh, I know what I need to do, Liz. I have a plan. Just listen."

He grew more and more agitated, and I couldn't help staring at the redness of his face, of his jaw.

"Look, I can do Leibowitz, I can do him too, I can destroy him."

He pushed the ON button.

"I can destroy Leibowitz."

I turned it off.

"Let it go, Will. Now."

"I can imitate him for you, his egghead and everything, look."

He pushed ON.

"Here's his schnoz, right? Ali told me, Ali told me, 'That dirty Jew, I'm going to stick him in the oven.' He told me that, you hear me."

I cut it off once and for all.

"That's what I imagine him saying, like he's paranoid, like Ali threatened me, you know."

Now he was laughing. He smelled like cooling meat.

"What do you say, Liz?"

My hand was stiff on the tape recorder, and now I felt like bawling.

"What are you doing, Will? Where are you going with all this?"

"Where am I going? Into a fucking coffin. Like us. Like you. You know what, you get on my fucking nerves. You're no fucking help. Get the fuck out of here. Go fuck yourself."

He was breathing hard, his nostrils flared, and he dragged me, his feet stamping the old carpet, to the door.

"Go on, you miserable cunt, go fuck yourself. I'm so fucking sick of you. If I were your boyfriend I'd find somebody else to fuck. Liz, you've gotten old."

He stopped in the doorway, he looked closely into my face.

"You've got wrinkles there, in your neck. It's ugly. I'm not interested in people with wrinkles, Liz. Not at all. People who are old, people who are sick. I don't want to lay eyes on you. Go get yourself fucked, while you still can."

He closed the door.

It was raining. I got wet. The courtyard of the hotel was gray, with cinder blocks and a few cloth sacks resting on the uneven ground among the puddles, near the Gare du Nord.

By the time I left the hotel, my hair was already soaked.

46

I couldn't think how to hold on to him anymore.

It's not that he pulled away. He stayed there in his gloom, more or less silent.

For more than ten years I'd been with this man. I knew him, that I knew.

The problem, I believed and feared, was that he didn't know me.

I didn't think he knew who I was, after ten years. What memories, what intuitions did he have? Could he anticipate even one of my gestures?

We never saw each other except in hotels and a dozen times abroad. I'd never cooked for him, he'd never seen my bathroom when it was a mess. Oh, yes, maybe he had, but just once.

Time passed, and so did his youth. Leibowitz was bald, he had hair on his ears, he didn't listen to me. More and more he seemed to feel an aversion to sex. It made me anxious. Every time I saw him, I wondered what I had to offer.

So I talked, and I said too much. I knew I wasn't young enough anymore. I'd have done anything for him, but I couldn't, I just couldn't be young for the rest of his life. He had told me, over and over again, that he was waiting for his children to move out.

I didn't dare tell him, "Jean-Michel, the younger one will be eighteen . . ."

He lay down. He caressed me, but that was all. I couldn't enjoy it. I couldn't concentrate.

"Jean-Michel, talk to me."

Something, I felt, disgusted him about his own fingers in contact with my skin, which made me afraid that he no longer loved the touch of it. What did I have beyond that?

I've always said too much.

It was raining. The bedroom was beautiful. This time there were hardwood floors. It was a good hotel.

To keep him from turning on the TV, I said, "I saw William."

I knew that would interest him.

"Miller?"

"I interviewed him."

I wanted to brag, I wanted to annoy him, to provoke him. I regret it, I regret it.

"What did he say? What is there for him to say? What's he scheming about now? He's over and done with."

He was talking to me. He had his hand on my stomach, and I didn't need to suck it in. I breathed.

I was speaking too quickly. "Easy, Liz. Easy."

Oh! He kissed me.

"What did he say? What did he tell you?"

I'd always known that William was a good way of keeping Leibo, like having a child so the father won't leave.

And I told him, embellishing slightly, what he said, and I told him yes, yes, he imitated Doumé, and he thought it was hysterical, joking around, about you, saying the Jews had invented AIDS. He said that. "It was the Jews who invented AIDS."

"He said that?"

"Yes." Instantly I regretted it.

"The bastard."

He held me.

"Did you record it?"

"Oh well, yes. But—"

"Good."

And I knew I was making a mistake, but I couldn't help it. I wanted him to hold me.

He started to make love to me, he apologized, he couldn't finish. "I'm sorry, I can't."

"Leibo—"

"It's this business of—that bastard! How can he talk that way. You know my father died because of him."

"Leibo . . ."

He didn't cry. If he had cried I could have held him.

I was nothing to him now. I had been a thread stretched toward something that was about to disappear, I was clinging to one side of him, and as far as that went, I knew, I had become almost entirely irrelevant. I understood.

Sitting on the bidet, I knew he was going to leave me.

"Leibo . . ."

It had stopped raining, and Leibowitz offered to buy me a drink. Behind his face lay something guilty. He touched the bridge of his nose.

He was going to tell me, he was just holding it inside.

47

Doum came to see me the next morning. Wearing a leather jacket, freshly shaven, he came to ask how I was. I was fine.

He coughed, and came out with it.

"I need the tape," he said.

That was the last time, I think, he ever sat on the cherry red sofa.

"The tape?"

"The recording. You need to give it to me."

I was wearing a cache-coeur, I was thirty-five. I looked at this old friend of mine, and could see how impatient he was to end things.

"The tape of my interview with Will?"

"Yes."

"What do you want to do with it?"

"It's time to end it, Liz. To have it over and done with."

"End it with Will? But isn't that all over already . . ."

"Come on."

"Why? He doesn't represent anything anymore, Doumé, you and Leibo have won."

The sky was still blue. Dominique told me to come with him, and he took the car. The air whistled by, the boulevards were wide, he drove me toward Port-Royal. Passing the Jardin du Luxembourg, near the end of boulevard Saint-Michel, I saw the big buildings and the sudden immense empty space that opened behind us. And I said, "You want me to give you the tape so you can use it against him?"

He held out a box of blackcurrant candies and answered yes.

He gave a tight smile. "I want him to shit himself, he'll get scared, and that will be the end of it. He's made so much trouble, and now we can crush him for good. And turn the page."

He stopped the car.

"Where are you taking me?"

He double-parked, then hesitated. "We can't stop here. There's no parking."

He pulled out, found a place and backed into it, then he fed three coins into the meter at the corner of the avenue.

"There's someone I want you to meet."

We had to go through a courtyard of thick gravel and into a dark staircase, finding the irregular red tiles with our feet, then climb another two floors, clinging to the creaky old wooden railing. Everything was clean, and I had the impression—

He stood back so I could go in first . . . "I believe you've met Richard Winter?"

It was obvious this wasn't his first visit. I wiped my shoes on the mat.

My God, the man was so thin. He'd shaved, and the bones of his face poked out from under his papery, peeling skin. He said hello, and his voice—I had to look at his lungs to make sure it was actually coming from there.

Doum sat down on the kitchen chair. No doubt he came there often. He knew the house, he flung out his hand in the man's direction.

"Richard Winter was a 'friend' of William's. The William you know. Do you remember hearing about him, about the doctor?"

The man had gray skin and a dry mouth. He offered me a glass of chocolate milk. I noticed the spots on his hands. He took a deep breath after every sip. There was something the matter with his throat, I noticed when he walked past me, but I couldn't tell what.

"They sent me home for a little while."

He poured a bit more milk for me and smiled. "It's nice of you to come see me. I don't have much time left. I feel it there—everywhere."

He pointed all over his body, he was insistent, he lifted his T-shirt. I heard myself say, "Oh my God!" and I covered my mouth. His stomach.

There wasn't enough light in the apartment. I was suffocating, literally.

Having rejected the idea of prevention, he had begun treatment too late.

Richard Winter patted Doumé's shoulder. "Luckily, Dominique was there for me, so was Stand. They supported me. They come every day. They're—they do so much to help me out." He sucked his dry tongue. "It's enough, as long as I don't fall apart completely." His teeth were yellow.

"A doctor like me—ironic, isn't it?"

I remembered William's story.

"Hasn't William come to see you?"

"No, no. He didn't want to see me anymore. I haven't heard anything from him. He just dropped me, completely, the moment he found out."

Dominique didn't say anything, he looked away across the kitchen. It was unbearable.

When Richard looked at me, even his eyes were hollow.

"It was an idiotic thing to do, which makes the whole thing idiotic. That's what I want people, young people, to know. You do something like that on a whim. Bang. Idiotic."

He breathed.

"If I could turn back the clock, I wouldn't think twice. I'd never do it again."

I wished I could look away, there was still something alive in his eyes.

"I'm going to die."

What could I say?

"Doumé, please," I murmured. "I understand. Let's go."

"There's no rush. We have all the time in the world. Don't you want to talk more, with Richard?" He smiled. "Finish your milk."

Richard fell silent, his eyes unfocused but still staring in my direction. I couldn't drink it, I had to drink it, as fast as possible. The apartment was so somber, he was so somber, the milk was so cold.

This lasted ten minutes, a very long time.

I looked sideways, at the wallpaper in the corridor, I took Richard's hand. He wouldn't let go of mine. I cried out, ridiculously, and hated myself for it. He was like a zombie.

"Dominique," I begged him, "we have to go."

He remained in the doorway, on the threshold, brown, gray. Dominique looked unconcerned, he toyed with the car keys in the left pocket of his flannel trousers.

The car. I wanted to be in the car. Now. Dominique . . . I implored him. His lips. They were like dust. He still wouldn't let go of my hand.

"I'll be back in a couple of days," Dominique said.

I wanted to go down, I wanted to be walking down the stairs.

He was still standing there, gray.

I wept. I didn't want to, but I did. "What can I do?" I said stupidly.

Dominique was heartless. He took his time opening the door of the building, letting me see the sky, which was still blue above the inner courtyard and its gravel.

"Liz, I need the tape."

He had to put me in the car now, you see.

LIFE

48

William had walked down every street of the Sixth Arrondissement, hands balled in his pockets. He was penniless.

When he asked his old friends, the young queers, to help him—there was no one. "Fuck it," he said. "It's one thing or another. Either they're wrecked because they got the disease or they're dead or they hate me": nobody knew him anymore, and all the worst things he'd done at one point or another to whoever had spent more than half an hour in his company now brought him scorn, at best, hate at worst. He was in pretty bad shape, but he didn't dwell on it. "Anyhow, I'm not going to fuck around with people I don't give a fuck about."

"Willie," I'd told him once, "I'll be the only one around to forgive you when your name can't bail you out."

He'd knocked on the door of every publisher, a manuscript under his arm. Three years before, they'd have bought the book without even looking at the title—today he made the rounds of those courtyards, from one *hôtel particulier* to the next, hidden away along boulevard Saint-Germain, beautiful buildings discreetly resting in the shade of a June day—and no one would see him, apart from apologetic secretaries.

He stood in the doorway. They told him, "You're welcome to leave it with me."

"No fucking way. I've only got the one copy. For whoever wants it."

"I'm sorry I can't help you, monsieur."

"Fucking hell."

Jean-Paul caught sight of him out the fourth-floor window, crossing the paved courtyard in a tight T-shirt, already slightly out of fashion, and moccasins. "Moccasins," he said, smiling. He filled his pipe. "The little bastard. To end up blaming the Jews for AIDS. It's disgusting and it's nonsense."

Michel had closed the office door. "It's true the guy's a Jew himself."

Jean-Paul nodded. "Maybe he has AIDS."

"Of course he does. Haven't you read Rossi's book? Oh . . . well, in any case, he was always unreadable."

Claude was the only one who would meet with him. He gave him a chair and told him to collect himself.

After a minute, Will seemed to have settled down. "Thank you, monsieur," he said.

Then he got excited talking about his novel. "It's not a novel," he started to say.

Claude cut him off. He'd been a publisher for thirty years. He didn't feel any particular animus toward Willie.

"William, I shouldn't have agreed to meet with you."

"Ah, right. Well, that's OK."

"No, it's not OK. No one is going to meet with you. No one will ever meet with you again. You have to—"

"Yeah, you're totally right."

"Let me explain."

"Explain? There's nothing to explain."

"Yes, there is. You have to forget about that novel of yours."

"My novel? It's fantastic. It's a work of genius. My master-piece. It's superphilosophical. You're going to—"

"Forget it. Forget all about it. You can chuck it in the trash. Nobody—you hear me, nobody—is going to publish it. You haven't accomplished anything since the first one—nothing at all. That's why I won't take it."

Claude had a double chin. Will watched his hands trace geo-
metric figures in the air. He was a wise man.

"OK."

"The others have reasons of their own. You can't stay here, in
Paris. There are . . . you know, people talk, and you're nobody
now. You ought to know, you ought to understand that I've gone
out of my way for you, just by meeting with you. I didn't have to
do it. I'm the only one who will. I'm a nice guy."

"OK."

Claude sighed. "No, it's not OK. It's like this: you didn't have
the means, you didn't have anything. It just happened to be the
right time. It was the moment. Now you've got to find a way to
make a living, do you understand what I'm saying?"

"OK, OK."

"All right. It was all a big mistake. Can you go back home?"

"Well, yeah."

"Where are you from? Up north, no?"

"Amiens."

"Ah, the cathedral."

"Yeah."

Claude rose heavily from his chair. "Did you do any kind of
training? Is there work you can go back to, back home?"

"Sure. I have plans. I've got loads of plans."

Claude nodded. "And you studied . . . sales?"

"Sales."

"Can you go back to that?"

And it all came back to Will: the white skies over Amiens,
the house near Étouvie, his brothers asking what was in the fridge,
his mother, his father, the castle of Compiègne, and the knights,
the kings who didn't exist, *Star Wars*, and the campus. The sheets.
Good sheets.

"You belong to something up there, it's better that way. It's
your home."

And Will sat there slack-jawed. It was over. He hadn't

done all those things for this. It wasn't exactly what he'd dreamed of.

"Do you have money for the train?"

William sniffled and looked away. "No, actually, I don't."

Claude fumbled in the pockets of his raincoat, which was hanging on the coat tree. He took out his wallet.

"Here." He closed Will's hand on something. "Now go."

"Yeah, right. I've got big plans, in Amiens. I know this guy at the business school."

"That's good. That's very good." Claude pushed him toward the door.

Once his visitor had left, he picked up the green folder holding the pages of the fat novel that William had accidentally left behind on the beige chair. He took the time to read the first few pages and he sighed vaguely to himself. It was shit. Completely without interest, you could see that right away, just as it had always been. He threw the whole thing away with a tiny pang in his heart.

I got a message from Will, who'd called from a phone booth. "Uh, hey, Liz, it's me. So I'm going back to Amiens. In fact, I'm in a big rush. I've got some serious plans. In fact, it's Claude's idea. I can't go into it, but it's great. Really great. I'm happy to see Amiens again, I mean, I'm really looking forward to that. So, well, thanks for everything. It was cool, Liz. Love you. All right now, ciao."

Until I bumped into Claude at a party, I really thought he'd found something to do. I let Claude have it—"It's because of Dominique and Jean-Michel." He'd published their book.

My God, to let him leave that way. I took a train the next day to go and find him.

It was early July, I was sure he must be living on the street. At best I expected to find him in a squat, near the station.

49

When I stepped out of the station I found myself facing the Perret Tower, which was under construction. I crossed the old town toward the cathedral. The esplanade was empty, the façade being renovated. There were an impossible number of stone blocks there, beside the water . . . I wandered north, I asked directions at a *bar-tabac*, a low redbrick building on the corner, identical to all the buildings around it. Just the kind of house in which Willie must have grown up, a little bit farther away.

I soon found the hospital.

I'd called his mother in the end. What a strange voice, buried in time. She didn't tell me much, but I knew where to find him.

It was the first time we'd ever spoken. "You're his girlfriend?" she had asked, in a weary voice. "He told me he had a girlfriend. Is that you?"

I said yes. I can't imagine what he'd told them, what they knew; they must have seen him at some point, on TV . . . But his mother was obviously not all there.

I asked for his room number, I took out my press card, I asked to speak to the head of the ward.

Patrice Schmitt invited me into his office. He didn't close the door. Nothing much was happening in the corridor, and that day the bustle of nurses and patients took place in relative silence.

He sat down. "His mother is the one who brought him here.

He was suffering from his first bout of encephalitis a month ago, but he's recovering now."

He opened the file. "In '96," he told me, "we had a patient dying of AIDS every two weeks. This year we've had two deaths." He smiled. "Unfortunately."

I sat where I was.

"For two, three years he didn't take anything. He never went in for any treatment. He didn't have a doctor. He behaved recklessly."

When he was staying with me, I had never seen him go to a doctor, not once. He didn't like doctors.

"Is it too late?"

Dr. Schmitt cleared his throat. "He has full-blown AIDS. So it will be over soon. Do you know much about it?"

"AIDS?"

"I mean, do you know, more or less, the three phases?"

I nodded vaguely.

"When he was infected, which from what he told me must have happened in '96 or '97, he must have felt the symptoms of an everyday viral infection. The viral load, the amount of the virus in the system, peaks six weeks after infection, then there's a drop-off. At the same time, the number of T4 white blood cells goes down, then rises back up."

He straightened his collar.

"He must have had fevers, a slight dilation of the tonsils, an inflammation of the throat, muscle aches, headaches, diarrhea, and nausea. These symptoms don't mean anything in themselves. But obviously he had them.

"He never got tested."

"Never? But—"

He shook his head.

"He lied to you. He knew in his gut. But he didn't have confirmation. Obviously, he does now."

"The latent phase can last for different lengths of time. In his case it lasted about eight years. It can last for up to ten. The white blood cells die at the same rate that the virus multiplies."

"And then?"

I was biting my thumbnail.

"He had no one tracking his case. It's hard to fathom. He didn't do anything. He wanted to shut his eyes to it. None of the people around him . . . well, he was in the pre-AIDS phase. What's called ARC, AIDS Related Complex. Obviously he wasn't doing well at his mother's. He's thin, he has lost fifteen percent of his body weight. I just want to warn you. So that's how things stand. His condition has stabilized. So you see, his viral load is still undetectable, and he still has a white cell count above four hundred per milliliter, but that's going to go down. It's going to drop.

"In the end it will drop below two hundred."

"Then what will happen?"

"Last time it was an inflammation of the brain. But you can never anticipate this kind of thing: it's a sudden alteration of the central nervous system. The virus affects the brain. Normally the blood-brain barrier isolates the brain and protects it, but it's permeable to white blood cells. The virus can travel to the brain via the microphages, which are like a kind of Trojan horse. They enter into the central nervous system, at first in a small quantity, then in larger quantities. They affect the neurons . . . And they bring along with them opportunistic infections. His chances of getting better are slim. We can stabilize him. But he could be overwhelmed at any moment, and then . . . Then he'll die.

"That's the thing, people in France still die of AIDS. It's a shame he didn't take care of himself. Obviously it's going to be, well, difficult."

I went to see him.

The first thing I noticed were the splotches and the lesions on his thin arms.

Stupidly, I thought they were tattoos, then I realized.

"Liz!" he called out. He was "too, too" happy to see me. He kissed me hello. "Hey there. This is so fucking cool."

He was sitting on his bed, eating applesauce.

"Hi, Will," I said and sat down beside him.

I glanced over at the white nightstand. He was drinking Gatorade.

"What's that stuff?"

"It's for diarrhea." And he laughed. "Oh, Liz, you should see the way I've been shitting! It's totally fucking crazy."

He wiped his mouth.

"How are you feeling?"

"Oh, I feel great. I feel super."

"Has—has your mother come to see you?"

"Yeah, sure she has. I've got lots of visitors, you know, kids I grew up with, all that, you can't imagine. It's really nice. It's cool."

I looked at him and I felt as though I were looking into a cracked jar of T4 cells, and that their level was falling right before my eyes.

"I feel fantastic, Liz. There's lots of stuff I need to do, obviously. Hey, I'm sorry, but when I eat I have to watch TV. Otherwise I barf. It's important. See, I have to stop and take deep breaths."

I passed my hand over his forehead.

"No, no, it's OK, I had a fever before, and they have this great stuff for sleeping, you sleep like a baby."

"What's that on your neck?" I leaned over delicately.

"What, that? That's nothing."

One or two ganglia, hypertrophied, and a bandage. He coughed.

He had these spots on his skin.

"Hey, it's cool. Did you see? On Tuesday they're rerunning *Return of the Jedi*. I can't believe it, I haven't seen it in so long. Do you remember?"

"No, Will, I never saw it."

"Really? Didn't we see it together? We should."

"I won't be here Tuesday. I have to work."

"Oh. Oh, right. Well, I'll see it with somebody else. One of the gang. But what are you doing here?"

I touched my own throat. "Me? What do you mean?"

"Liz? Is that you? What are you doing here?"

He hadn't finished his soup or his banana.

The doctor reassured me. "He blanks out sometimes, because of the encephalitis."

When I left, Will was excited, but he was obviously tired. "You know, Liz, I'd like to become a doctor, because . . ." He whispered in my ear, "I have all these theories, but I don't want to talk too much about them, not with people listening."

"Oh, really."

"Yeah, really. I'm telling you, I've been studying it. And you know what, it isn't HIV that causes AIDS."

"What do you mean? What are you talking about?"

"There's no connection, I'm telling you. Nobody can prove it. Because you know it's political, making us believe that, they want to make the queers take AZT, a transcriptase inhibitor, you know, and the AZT was poisoned—I mean it—so they could suppress all the queers."

"I don't follow you, Will."

"You don't follow? Shh. I know it. The medicines were poisoned from the beginning. You see the irony. I refuse to take them.

"HIV is good for queers, it's just good, but meanwhile they tell us no, no, the virus is what gives you AIDS, AIDS is viral, right, so you need to take AZT, but in fact AZT is what actually gives you AIDS, that's why they all died. But not me—hey, you know, I never took it. I won't take the medication. And . . . you know what? You know where they make it? Shh. It's the Jews, I'm telling you, the Jews are the ones who own the shares in the company that makes AZT. Now do you get it? You have to follow the money, right?

"I won't take the drugs."

He smiled, but he was tired; his skin was slightly swollen and was turning purple on his nose and below his left cheek.

"But . . . but, Will, you never took AZT, and you . . ."

"Well, exactly. That's why I don't have AIDS. That's the difference."

I smiled sadly.

His eyes lost their focus.

"I think you're tired, Will. You're just tired."

"Yeah . . . I mean no. It's not that."

I watched him for a minute as he lay there in the silence. He was handsome, when he didn't move around too much. His face seemed distorted against the white sheet, as if his bones were growing despite him, in a slightly unruly way. His thin skin, too thin, stretched like a plastic film over his cheekbones. In places his skin, his very dear skin, my God, his skin like a baby's was so cracked, worn, and creased, shot through by a cruel web of red capillaries, that my eyes filled with tears. His poor skin. What was happening to it? I pinched my nose, to control myself. He kept stifling belches that smelled faintly of vomit, he looked catatonically at the television, he nodded; for a moment I thought he was waiting for Doumé to appear on the screen.

My poor little friend. I didn't even kiss him or caress him. Later, on the train back home, I wished I had. I think his system was falling apart, it made me afraid, it wasn't really possible to do anything for him—anything at all. He was a wreck just waiting to collapse.

I ought at least to have kissed him when I left.

"I'll be back next week," I told him.

"No problem, Liz," he answered. "Everything's great. Everything's cool."

50

I knocked at the door. He had forgotten to come and get me.

"Liz! I completely forgot to come get you."

He kissed me. He was well.

He invited me in.

"You see, everything's in its place. I've settled in."

He'd been there several months.

"Don't you miss Paris?"

"No. Not a bit. I do my shopping over there, on the right, at the little grocery. It's nice. Like an old man. There's a garden, come, I'll show you the garden. Did you see the rosebush? Look, it's coming back. It's coming back."

Then we had a drink in the upstairs salon with its wood paneling. It was nice and cool there, despite the heat wave.

"I'm really sorry not to have picked you up at the airport. Something came up, you know, a piece of business."

"No, no, don't worry about it. There was a hiker on his way to Calenzana. He dropped me off down at the hikers' cabins. I went through the village. It's beautiful. Really beautiful. It wasn't a problem at all."

"From here, there's a hiking trail that crosses the entire island."

"Have you done it?"

"We did it every summer with my father. You have to be in shape."

He drank his bourbon.

"I think I'll do it in September."

The doorbell rang.

He went downstairs. He was the only one who lived there. I stayed where I was. I looked out the window at the horizon, at the foothills and the sea. It was dry, pure, and very clean. On the walls, books. I heard whispering downstairs.

I waited five minutes, then I heard voices. I leaned over the banister at the top of the mahogany-colored stairs. I shouldn't have looked. It was Alain—the former head of the Cuncolta Naziunalista, one of the leaders of the armed wing of the party, sidelined ever since Tralonca and mixed up with the Brise de Mer, the Toulon mafia. When I flew out of Paris, that morning, the police were searching for him at L'Île-Rousse.

I went back to my chair. Dominique came up, he introduced us. "A childhood friend, he'll be staying here tonight."

I must have raised an eyebrow.

"We have always had our differences, but he's my guest. And that is sacred." He smiled. "Man, Alain, we used to say some crazy things in this room, didn't we."

The same Alain closed his cell phone. He was bald, his nose aquiline. He shook my hand. There was something macho about him, but also something rather sweet.

He turned to Dominique and punched him lightly in the belly. "You let your beard grow, Dominique. You know you're going to end up just like your father."

Then he turned back to me. "His father was quite something, not the sort of person you forget." There was a silence. "Many people came to his funeral. Men who would have killed each other shook hands over his coffin, you know. What a life he led. He was the kind of man who touched the lives of everyone he met, though afterward of course they may have gone their own way."

51

Having begun the conference circuit with Dominique, Leibowitz now gave his talks alone.

Françoise, a former student of his four years behind me, now working in the central office of the UMP, invited him to the annual convention: this was just at the moment when the French right was choosing between Jacques Chirac and Nicolas Sarkozy. No one knew yet which way Leibowitz would cast his vote. At the time most people expected him to go with Sarkozy, but he was a "loyalist" to the head of state and his support was nonnegotiable.

Leibowitz closed his cell phone. He'd just found someone to perform his nephew's bar mitzvah.

He climbed to the lectern, he made a little sign to the sound technician. He always had a word for the little people, in honor of his father.

This wasn't really a talk anymore, but a political speech. He smiled at the auditorium. This took place in Colmar.

"I was the first victim of what you might call a cleansing process—though I'd never dare to describe it as ethnic."

Laughter.

Thanks to the anti-Semitism of French elites, he had been the target of an intellectual witch hunt. And today, he, the Cassandra—well, all you had to do was look at the germs of the riots in the Parisian banlieues, the riots that Ali Hassam called "positive signs of consciousness." All you had to do was consider that members of the Assemblée, in attendance this evening, had found it necessary to pass a law against anti-Semitic acts. In the year 2005, sixty years after the Shoah, wasn't it inconceivable that one would have to write a law to protect the Jews of France?

Leibowitz painted a portrait of France in decline—he who had predicted this decline ten years earlier. Today all the experts had come around. We were living in a nation that was culturally sclerotic, obsessed with victimhood, a nation that went around projecting itself phantasmagorically on all kinds of so-called victims, seeing its own weakness in them: the systematic victimization of the Palestinians, the anti-American speechifying of a José Bové . . . And today a "friend" of Bové like M. Ali found himself spearheading the most recent riots in the banlieues. "What will we do when the Intifada comes to the Parisian banlieues—will we keep blaming Israel?"

He was still an intellectual. He was listened to with interest in the light of his regained prestige. The neoconservatives, certain pro-American politicians and Sarkozy supporters, genuinely found coherence in what he said.

Leibowitz beat his fist against the table.

"Does this strike you as delusional? I, for one, won't cross sides. Nor am I the only one. Times have changed. We must not be afraid of our beliefs, of our origins, of our convictions. We are Westerners, we have American friends, we believe in a God, and we reject communism just as we reject the green fascism of the Islamic extremists.

"Raymond Aron, our forefather, used to say . . ."

Then Leibowitz put forward his panoramic understanding of French culture in its entirety. Everybody clapped.

He drank a glass of water. In the front row, a man in his fifties was nodding in agreement, thin, tall, and reserved.

Leibowitz lowered his tone at the end.

"I have been affected, personally, by the madness of the minoritarian majorities who took control of our country, our country that belongs to *all* of us, as members of the Republic, whatever our origins may be . . .

"Some of you know this document . . . It has to do with one of M. Hassam's friends, his boyfriend to be exact. It bears a terrible witness and is taken from an interview made some time ago.

"Here is the sort of thing that one can say today, in our country, with impunity . . ."

He pointed toward the soundman, who nodded and hit PLAY. The voice crackled badly, it echoed strangely in the room.

"The Jews are the ones who invented AIDS. It was the Jews, those fucking shitbags, who invented AIDS in their laboratories after the Yom Kippur War. It was a biological weapon. That's the truth, there's proof. I can destroy Leibowitz. Here's his schnoz, right? Ali told me, Ali told me, 'That dirty Jew, I'm going to stick him in the oven.' He told me that."

Silence.

"Obviously I have decided to take legal action against M. Hassam through my lawyer, M. Malone."

He pinched his nose and ended his speech: "This is where our country finds itself. It is quite sad and, as I have always said, it is in our culture, not in barbarism, that we must seek the origins of this malaise, and it is in our culture that you must, that we must, take action, and react. Thank you."

There was sustained applause. Not everyone agreed with everything he'd said, but many did.

Françoise came and took him by the arm.

Alexandre, the prefect, came up to congratulate him, and Malone gave him a nod from the audience. Leibowitz let out a deep breath. He was safe.

Françoise remained on his arm, and Alexandre told him:

"I want you to meet Jérôme Deniau, he knows Nicolas well, but he has his connections at the Élysee. You'll like him."

The elegant man, slender, with a shining skull, shook his hand while Françoise tapped his other arm.

"I'm won over. We are all very impressed."

"Thank you."

52

I went back to see Willie, and I took him for a walk in the Hortillonnages. Dr. Schmitt had given his permission.

"Just don't tire him out too much."

I asked whether he'd had any visitors.

"His mother, I've seen her three times, and then you. He strikes me as very much alone."

It was summer, and the sun was high in the sky. William's condition was relatively stable. He had his blank moments, and his T4 level was now hovering near two hundred. It was the moment that opportunistic illnesses would begin to spread in him, I knew that.

He had trouble walking, and we stopped next to the little pond.

A couple of dogs ran back and forth, each with a stick in its mouth. Several young couples strolled past.

We sat a few steps farther on, on the benches, under a small Japanese-looking shelter that rose up at the edge of the water, and the sun shone down.

William's eyes were very round, and he bore no resemblance to the muscular Apollo he'd so recently been. He was short of breath. He was counting on his fingers.

"That makes five, Liz, one for each finger, like a ring, you see, when I think back on the men I've loved. Is that a lot, do you think? I mean, really, isn't that a lot? Now I realize, looking back, that they're all kind of the same, in a certain way: Guillaume, the one I fell in love with in Amiens, and then my boss. And then Dominique. And Richard, what happened to him? And then Ali too. It's strange to put them all on the same plane, as equals, as if they were all floating on the surface of the water, you know. Like those Japanese paper things. Everything's turned to hate. They all hated me in the end. Except for Guillaume— but then, that wasn't true love."

I took his hand so I could see it—he was looking away. He had liver spots like an old woman, and a bulging vein. His skin was dry, gray and green, gray and gray. He didn't smell good, to tell the truth. He was always wringing his hands. He had pains in his extremities and his joints.

At every second, I watched his movements or his breathing for a sign. What would crack first, when his system finally shut down? Would it be the lungs, cancer, tuberculosis? His body was open wide, unprotected, and soon all the filth of the world would clog it up, like an engine left in the open air that can no longer be cleaned.

With a cough he reached into the pocket of the windbreaker I had bought him and took out a ragged little paper doll.

"Do you know what this is?"

I didn't.

"It's Dominique . . . Do you have a needle?"

"A needle?" I rummaged in my handbag. "I have a safety pin, if you like."

He smiled, it was as if he had no more lips, he widened his eyes, and pow, he stuck the pin right through the paper figurine. I laughed.

"Don't laugh. It's serious, you know. Superserious. It's voodoo. It works. There's a complete theory behind it and it's true."

"Oh, really?"

"Yes." He spoke into my ear. "Shh. Don't say anything. I have a plan. I'm going, I'm going to get myself killed. You'll see, I'm going to die, I'm going to get killed. And then"—he giggled—"you'll see, they're going to accuse Dominique. He's going to get it this time. I've been thinking it over for a while."

I looked at the water, and the cattails.

"Really."

"Yes, totally. I have contacts with M. Malone, a good lawyer. He's going to get a killer for hire, but it's like in a thriller, everything's slowly going to point to Dominique, and then he's going to be in deep shit, I'm telling you, he's really going to be in deep shit. I'll be dead. But I'm going to drag him down with me. He's going to lose everything—everything. What do you think?"

I didn't say anything.

"Hey, don't go telling him. Don't rat me out, do you promise? Shit, don't do that to me."

"No, no. That sounds like a good idea, Will."

"Doesn't it? It sounds super. It sounds excellent."

In that moment, when he clicked his tongue against his palate, with difficulty, trying to swallow, that was when I saw it.

He had these strange marks on his tongue. It's what Schmitt had said: oral hairy leukoplakia. All along the top of it, cracking. And on his palate, my God, purple fissures, he must have wanted to scratch them. A Kaposi's sarcoma.

Kaposi. 1872.

A decomposition, blood-red, in his mouth, like the severed head of a skinned rabbit, where his palate ought to be. Swollen.

"'S cool," he slurred. "My teeth have stopped hurting. 'S the medications, I don't take them.

"No, no," he curled up. "'S because I hurt all over. That compensates."

They were doing what they could for his pain. He had the beginnings of hepatitis. All his defenses were falling apart. His poor soul was crumbling like a dam. His tightly shut little heart, which had been, as he would have said, maxed out in this fucked-up world, opened all the way up, bleeding and unprotected. And everything that surrounded it, like spores, came to burrow into his body, to swell it, deform it, undo it, and tear it to pieces. His body . . . When he arrived in Paris, when the Berlin Wall came down, he'd looked pretty good as long as he watched his posture.

He was always bent over, and there was something too fragile now about his bones.

"Are you coming?"

He had pricked himself with the safety pin, so that a bead of blood rose up on the too-visible vein on the back of his forearm.

"Will, what are you doing?"

With the head of the pin he dabbed a drop of blood onto the paper figurine.

"It's voodoo. I'm infecting him. So he'll die. He's going to die. It's already in the cards."

"Will, Dominique is already positive."

"Oh." He looked at the little red dot on the paper. "Will he keep living when I'm dead? Is he immortal?"

"No, Will."

"You know, I think about him a lot. Not an hour goes by that I don't think of him. I still have plans, believe me. *It ain't over till it's over.* And then you can do it for me, if he's still living afterward, you never know, you can take care of him for me, right?"

"Sure, Will."

He got up, and we went back. The Hortillonnages, those winding little canals in a lush green landscape of underbrush and woodland, swarming with summer life in the corner of the old town . . . From there we wandered toward the Jardins de l'Évêché. We came out and I took him back to the hospital at four o'clock.

I touched him cautiously, and I almost seemed to feel the

virus through his pores, under his skin, in his veins, up his spinal fluid all the way to his brain and in his bulging eyes, bursting forth like a bad outbreak of acne, full of a fatal sebum.

I picked up a stone for him, as if we were going to play hopscotch there on the road, past the wooden bridge, by the curb.

"It's cool," he said. He spoke less and less.

"Did you go for walks here, when you were little?"

"Oh, no. No."

"Too far from home?"

"Oh, no. We just didn't go for walks much. We didn't really go out."

When I left, he asked me simply, "I have him this time, don't I?"

"Who?"

"Him."

"I don't know, Will."

"Huh. He's fucked anyhow. He's in deep shit, and I'd be very surprised if he gets out of it this time. He's in very deep shit."

53

He looked wonderful, he was beaming, he told me, "It just gets better and better," and he burst out laughing.

I'd gone back to Corsica, just for the weekend, with no purpose but to beg him.

"Doumé, this is it, he's going to die, you ought to go see him at least. No matter what happened, the two of you—"

He had come to get me in an apple green Renault 4L. He drove slowly.

"I'm so wrapped up in prevention, Liz. I have to look after myself."

Dominique had his life, I know that. "I'm finished with the community, it's over for me." He had lots of friends, a life of tranquility. "And I want to fall in love again someday, I'll find someone, it's not too late. I've lost so many years, ten years at least, so much time. Now it's over."

"Dominique, he's dying."

He lifted his hands from the wheel and let them fall back. It was a gorgeous day.

"What can I do?"

He opened the window.

"Look, Elizabeth, what do you want me to say? It's too bad. He had plenty of warning, we all did."

He downshifted and started gently up the slope that led to the village.

"He's out of my life, out of our life. It's over. We'll forget all about him, and I have to say, it's better that way. The guy was poison. Let him go back to his family, to his own people, let him die in peace where he came from with the people who love him. That's it. I don't wish him any harm. Let him do the best he can, that's life, Liz."

"Doumé."

I was shaking.

"You're really getting worked up over this, Liz. Look at yourself, you're destroying yourself. For Christ's sake, you have to take care of yourself, you ought to get out and do something. You spend too much time thinking about other people. Look how far you're taking this. Oh, stop, now you're crying."

We were there.

"Doumé, you really don't want to go see him?"

He'd let himself grow a short beard, he was in good health, he wore his old shirt; he let three seconds pass. "No. No, I don't. That's all. What do you want me to say? I don't give a fuck about him. We took him down, we had to, for the sake of morality, for the record. He wanted to push things all the way, and there you go. There you go. I don't feel any hate toward him, honest to God, it's true. Not anymore. And he doesn't mean anything to me now. Nothing. And there you have it."

He shrugged, he got out of the car, with his finger he rubbed a sickly plant he was bringing back to life.

I knew for a fact that I was behaving this way because I myself was in bad shape. I had no idea where I'd end up.

"It wasn't his fault, Liz. He didn't know the codes, he didn't have the key, he had no way of knowing, it wasn't his fault. It's sad. But he was such a little shit. And I just hope his soul will end up finding some kind of peace, and that everyone will forget all about it. To tell the truth . . ."

He spread his arms, his fingers were level with the mountains against the blue sky.

"I don't give a fuck. At all. I never even think about the guy. William Miller. No, sorry. I'm sorry for him. Let him do the best he can, let him enjoy whatever he's got left to enjoy, and let's hope he doesn't suffer too much. That's it."

I walked alongside him.

"I'll take you up this way, this afternoon. You see that big rock up there? We'll be able to see the entire bay, and over there, where the forest is, we'll see the groves of oaks. I'll show you. It's amazing. Take the water bottle. We'll need two water bottles and walking shoes. It will do you good, you'll see. Rest, and then we'll go."

He was a good walker, with a long stride; he had fallen back into the habits of his youth and he was more or less the man he must have been before I knew him, with more confidence and less devouring curiosity about life on the other side of the sea, on the continent—and this restored human being who walked before me no longer held the slightest interest for me. At least, no more than any other man.

In any case, I don't suppose I mattered to him either—insofar as I ever did. I was an old friend, one of many, a guest just like the others.

You realize that you've only been close to another person because of something else, some other thing, and when that goes, so does the feeling.

54

The Leib took me out to dinner: "There's something I need to tell you," he announced. "It's hard. I don't know how to say it.

"You and I . . ." He stopped, he drank, he collected himself. "Has it ever really worked between us?"

As he lowered his glass I saw his head through it, deformed, amber-colored, reassuring and warm, but bald.

"It's a question of being faithful. It took me so long to understand."

I told him I had never stopped loving him.

"I love Sara, Liz. Being faithful . . . It's only now that I can understand . . ."

It was always a bad sign with the Leib when he couldn't finish his sentences.

He pinched the bridge of his nose very hard, the way he always did when he was about to cry, and he told me, "It took me until now to understand the meaning of what I wrote, you know, in *Fidelity* . . . And you . . . I . . . I've cheated on you, Liz. Oh, I must be such a monster, Liz, I can't go on this way, I've changed so much I . . . I don't even know what I am anymore . . ."

He was sobbing.

"You haven't changed, Leibo," I murmured. I was speaking through a wall of cotton.

"You're going to hate me now, Elizabeth. I'm leaving you. It's over."

"I understand," I told him.

"We were wrong . . . No, not wrong, we couldn't have been wrong all these years. But things have changed between us. It only has to do with you and me. It's over, there's nothing left. I only want you to take care of yourself now. You need to do something for yourself, you're still so young. You deserve better than this. You understand, I can't do this to you."

"I understand, I understand," I repeated. And nevertheless I finished my dinner.

55

That September, the president of the Republic slightly reshuffled his cabinet, for he wished to reorient the French government toward the interests and preoccupations of civil society, in light of the recent failure of the referendum on the European Constitution.

Renaud Donnedieu de Vabres, the Minister of Culture, went back to take his seat as the member for l'Indre-et-Loire in the Assemblée, where he occupied the vice presidency of the Committee on Foreign Affairs.

Jean-Michel Leibowitz was named to replace him, as had been expected for several weeks.

56

On August 5, though the date has no particular significance, Will died.

A profound immunodeficiency, due to the virus, had just begun to express itself: opportunistic infections had flourished and then, according to the doctor, a latent or perhaps dormant infection, which had been controlled by the immune system, had been reactivated. There were signs of herpes, or shingles. I hadn't seen that.

He had suffered from a new outbreak of encephalitis in July. The prognosis had been uncertain and they never figured out what the pathogen was that attacked his brain. Very dehydrated, he had fallen out of bed not long afterward, just as his condition had begun to stabilize. They had forgotten to install bars around his bed.

He was alone. I was in Corsica and his mother wasn't visiting.

They transferred him to the orthopedic ward for an operation with general anesthesia, meant to set the fracture. Poor Will, what a torment it must have been, he must have felt so disoriented, and there they were shuttling him from one ward to the next. From what they told me, he had stopped saying much, he looked utterly stunned.

"He wasn't too much of a . . . nuisance to you?" I asked the nurse, because I worried, knowing how difficult he could be and seeing him in my mind's eye, him with his foul temper, always ready to insult women, to say some nonsense, this or that and then the opposite, endlessly and about everything, playing the mad genius.

"Oh, no. He was always well-behaved, even—don't take this the wrong way—a little bit dull. He kept himself to himself—but what do I know?"

"Which side of the bed did he fall from?" I asked, for no reason.

"I don't remember. He wanted to go pee. Because of his bladder. He couldn't control himself anymore, you see. He was ashamed of it, but we always kept his sheets clean."

They set the fracture. Then Schmitt prescribed T-20 as part of the treatment, to slow the replication of the HIV.

He was always bumping his head. And his body, he'd become so thin, he insisted on letting his hair grow long, but with his sores and his edemas, you understand . . .

He fell into a coma at the end of July, they pronounced him dead eight days later.

57

She wouldn't let me in. The door groaned, and she peeked out.

"Who are you?"

"It's me. I'm Elizabeth, William's friend, you know."

I was dressed all in black.

"Oh, yes."

We went together to the cemetery, northwest of Amiens.

I had got my license, I drove the car, she didn't speak. She said nothing. She kept swallowing. She was already an old woman.

Rue Saint-Maurice, the big park-cemetery of the Madeleine—would Willie have liked it? Maybe no, maybe yes. It was a gray day.

He might have said: Look at all those stones . . . and he would have liked it.

He might have said: It stinks of death here. He would have hated it. Who knows?

There were even fewer people than I'd have thought.

One of his brothers was there, I don't know which. I didn't even catch his name. He hadn't shaved. His father shook my hand.

"Thank you for what you did for my son. I'm not sure he was worth it."

He was tall, broad-shouldered, with a smile that worked on only one side of his face. He and the mother didn't say hello.

They brought the coffin. I watched them prepare the corpse and close it. William had made a will, years before. Oh, nothing much. He just asked to be incinerated.

Obviously Judaism doesn't recognize cremation, and I had asked the mother her advice. She didn't even know what it meant. I had to explain.

"Ashes?"

"Yes."

"Well, if that's what he wanted."

As long as it's not too expensive, said the father.

There I was in my suit, hands resting on my belly, standing in this large cemetery so full of headstones. All the great nineteenth-century families of Amiens had been laid to rest there, in rich and ornate tombs, in the shade of tall trees.

Willie's coffin was made of paper. Or rather, of a paper compound, lightweight, with the look more or less of a normal coffin, eighteen millimeters thick.

I had a sort of cramp in my stomach. We were there, all four of us, at the door of the crematorium.

The path was quiet, the heather-colored horizon bathed the place in a light that was steady, then flickered, shining rosy on the gray stones and under the tall trees.

At the door a kindly white-haired old man respectfully offered us pamphlets from the Flanders-Artois-Picardy Inter-Regional Association of Cremationists. I read only the last sentence on the grainy, recycled sheet of green paper:

"In order to make cremation—which is nonpolluting and leaves the earth for the living—free for all, as for several years it has been in Denmark, the great and beautiful family of cremationists must band together, united by ties of brotherhood and friendship, to create a new humanism before death."

It was a fine goodbye for Willie, I was sure he'd have liked it, and with his usual enthusiasm I could hear him taking up the cause: "No, but it's clear, Liz, cremation's the best, it's like Spinoza says. It's lame sticking people in the ground like a bunch of peasants. I mean, we come from cities, we've never set foot on the earth, and now we're supposed to go back to it? Please. Fire's clean. And then you end up in the air, thin air, it's fantastic, it's the future, Liz, it's our element, it's where we're all headed."

I thought of that, my head bowed in the crematorium, sitting on a chair. They had just put the coffin into the oven, heated to 900 degrees centigrade.

We didn't see anything—a red-orange-yellow glow in the semidarkness of the room. Will's father tapped his foot, the mother remained curled in on herself, the brother made his apologies and left. From across the room he mouthed to me, Thank you.

The attendant came over. "Would you like to say a few words, or pray, or play some music?"

In his will he had asked that we play the song "Si j'étais un homme." I'd bought the CD online. I hesitated, then took it out of my bag.

They played the song twice, all the way through.

His father laughed and laughed. He was having a ball.

Then the silence returned. His mother hadn't understood any of it.

It lasted an hour and a half.

The cemetery was romantic, the trees magnificent, the sun still high in the sky. I put on my sunglasses and walked a short way on the gravel.

The father came to speak with me. He had the same lower face as William, and he fiddled with his belt buckle.

"You know, that's the way it is. Not everyone succeeds in life, mademoiselle. It's a jungle. William was a weakling. William was weak. I could tell right away. Right away. It was plain. His mother . . . He was the runt, you understand, all that. He wet the bed. He wet the bed."

I didn't know what to say. He was the kind of man who shuts you up just by speaking.

"But hey, that's the way it is. Things are tough all over; things are tough all over. He wasn't much good. He wasn't much good. What exactly did he do for a living, anyway?"

"I . . ."

"Come on. Look. Don't kid yourself." He spread his arms, gesturing toward the big empty space all around us amid the gray tombstones. "There's nobody here. There's nobody here when he's dead. He didn't do anything. He didn't do anything, there's no one. That's just how it is. I mean, please, no one's going to cry over him. The best ones manage, it's the best ones who get ahead. But him, well, no. Hey, the kid wasn't much good."

The attendant interrupted, carrying the urn in both hands.

The residue of his calcium. Ashes, sifted in a can, soldered shut and in an urn.

The father said, "Oh, no. No way. Not for me. I won't take it."

The attendant went on politely, "He must have had some dental fillings, those would have been vaporized."

And stupidly, I looked at the sky, at the smoke that poured from the chimney and the clouds in the white sky.

The undertaker said, "No, that's not him."

I gave the urn to the mother, and the father said goodbye. He now lived in Boulogne.

"There's a temporary storage facility, if you need to think about it for a few months. You can scatter them in the Garden of Memory . . ." He gestured to a space on our right.

And I drove the mother to her house near Étouvie.

She got out of the car, she said nothing to me, and she disappeared into her house.

The ashes of William's body are somewhere, on a shelf, on some piece of furniture, in the darkness of the quaint house near Étouvie, the house where he was so stifled throughout his adolescence:

"You have no idea, Liz, what a dump it was, and my mother, it smelled of dust, the blinds were drawn at noon every Sunday, my lungs were completely contracted, you know. It was so small, it was the only world I knew, I was buried, the world was so tiny, dark, dusty, and dead, like in a box, you see, a tiny little box. You don't know how happy I was to get out of there, to breathe, to live, to have fun outside . . . You just have no idea."

I drove away and never went back.

THE BEST
IN MEN

58

It's time for me to leave you. Here I am, in the end, as you know, alone; cut off from my men, my three men, I worry I'll wear out your patience.

.

In the end the connections among several beings last only for a certain culminating moment in life, and the strong feelings that rise up, joining three or four people together, to the point of obsession, come back down again and finally leave nothing in our memories except the form of a bell curve—which one must leave behind, just as it is. That's when you face the fact that there are billions of human beings and that we are only four among the billions. Faced with such proportions, humanity strikes you as rather dull, compared to the tiny cluster who have taken up the best years of your life.

And as you plunge back into the billions, shouldn't there be one single lesson to keep from this minuscule group? What wouldn't I give for a lesson and a voice that would tell me what to keep, among all the things lost and gone . . . Unfortunately, I don't see anyone else to tell me, no one but myself—and so I try.

.

It seemed to me that love between a man and a woman in those years, under certain conditions, in certain places, and among the best of us, became sad. Simply sad, depressive, like an actor in the great theater of Nature who has become too mindful of his text . . .

In those days there was something surprising and much happier, generally speaking, about men who loved one another, and about women too, no doubt, something finally grander, and more tragic. All that changed with time, more or less quickly, and the opposite may be true for our children—even if I don't have any (children, I mean).

I won't have any heir. I have never loved a heart the way I loved William Miller, all appearances against him notwithstanding—and I will never transmit any of that to another person. What will I keep of him—besides the things I've told you?

•

William loathed me; I know this isn't true.

I always thought he must have reserved, in the depths of his soul, a love that he never showed anyone. He departed then, far from our eyes, with all that was best about him intact in the pit of his stomach, after he'd cast his wickedness far and wide.

Jean-Michel Leibowitz swung back and forth, wildly, and what's left of him is some pirouettes of the spirit, a few decisions, several nosedives. He seems to have changed entirely, bewilderingly, but take one step back and you see him as he is, always the same, my lover.

William Miller sowed turmoil all around him, and never had within him any seed but the seed of goodness.

Dominique Rossi stands fast. He has done some things, he has fought to keep them from vanishing, and in his exhaustion he has entered a retirement that he must think richly deserved. Don't many of us share this fate?

And I, I don't know what to say for myself. Oh well, since I'm on my way out I'll let you say it.

Let's say that I fell somewhere between Leibo, Doum-Doum, and Willie. Between Willie and himself.

·

He was pure. In contact with the world, that makes for someone extremely dirty.

·

But there are plenty of faithful ways to be a traitor, and treacherous ways to be faithful.

You can do good badly, you can unlovingly make love, and you can do evil without wickedness. Nothing you do assures the manner in which you do it, or what you are—as we've seen.

·

And what was he? He was different, and everyone is different—so what's the big deal?

·

Dominique retired to the island where he came from, he has money and the feeling of having lived a useful life; Jean-Michel exposed himself to power, he deserves credit for that: he made himself a name and a reputation, he will have, for some years yet, people to defend and admire him, people to hate and attack him, he is *something*; while William, who didn't come from much, is nothing and is dead. I live, I go on, and when it's over for me, I don't think that much will be left behind—except, I suppose, for things involving *them*.

·

Someone who, like Willie, steps without any inheritance into the world of ideas and speeches has the advantage, for a brief moment, of appearing to be a genius, an original, and over time, as old habits reassert themselves, he becomes an idiot, an interloper—and then he must retreat to his old camp, where he no longer belongs.

•

Our origin reveals itself only slowly to be our destiny, and with some weariness, some relief, some fright, we come to understand it. The way we understand it depends on the way we first wanted not to understand it, and to be free.

•

Between the moment he left home and the moment when he went back, William must have been free in this sense, inwardly.

•

There are human beings whose value remains hidden away all their lives, and there is of course no way to verify that value, to measure it, to know if they are potentially extraordinary or mediocre, except to live in their company. Absent, far away, or dead, none of what is best about them remains visible to the outside world: the possibility, the incessant doubt that they might be much more, in fact, than what they are.

Human beings whose whole importance is on display, in the form of facts, achievements, speeches, because they speak up, because they act and work—death hardly takes anything from them; and it seems to me more and more that everything I found to admire in the world—ideas, works, acts and lives—must have come from men who were opportunists, the sort of men I know, most of whom would have left me cold and whom the occasion, seized at the right moment, made a sort of genius, in all fields of life.

•

Is the value of a man what he leaves behind—feelings, convictions, objects, images, and gestures—or is it what he keeps to himself?

No doubt those who leave a great deal, the ones who remain, have infinitely little left within them . . .

·

The men whose best part is not their hearts, but everything around them, their deeds, their words, and everything that follows from them, their parents, their heirs—they live on beyond themselves, their death is in the end only a detour in their long duration in our eyes.

As for the best part of men who keep the best within their hearts, for lack of any outlet, to the final hour, it lives and dies with them.

ACKNOWLEDGMENTS

Thanks to Jean Le Bitoux for his kindness, his help, and his advice.